RANDOM HOUSE

LARGE PRINT

Red
at
the
Bone

Red
at
the
Bone

Jacqueline Woodson

RANDOM HOUSE
LARGE PRINT

Copyright © 2019 by Jacqueline Woodson

Published in the United States of America by Random House Large Print in association with Riverhead Books, an imprint of Penguin Random House LLC, New York.

Cover design by Jaya Miceli

The Library of Congress has established a Cataloging-in-Publication record for this title.

ISBN: 978-0-593-15225-6

www.penguinrandomhouse.com/large-print-format-books

FIRST LARGE PRINT EDITION

Printed in the United States of America

10 9 8 7 6 5 4 3 2 1

This Large Print edition published in accord with the standards of the N.A.V.H.

for the ancestors, a long long line
of you bending and twisting

bending and twisting

Bro, how you doing? You
holding on?

Man, you know how it goes.
One day chicken. Next
day bone.

—Two old men talking

1

But that afternoon there was an orchestra playing. Music filling the brownstone. Black fingers pulling violin bows and strumming cellos, dark lips around horns, a small brown girl with pale pink nails on flute. Malcolm's younger brother, his dark skin glistening, blowing somberly into a harmonica. A broad-shouldered woman on harp. From my place on the stairs, I could see through the windows curious white people stopping in front of the building to listen. And as I descended, the music grew softer, the lyrics inside my head becoming a whisper, **I knew a girl named Nikki, I guess you could say she was a sex fiend.**

No vocalist. The little girl didn't know the words. The broad-shouldered woman, having once belted them out loud while showering, was now saved and refused to remember them. Iris wouldn't allow them to be sung and Malcolm's brother's sweet seven-year-old mouth was full. Still, they moved through my head as though Prince himself were beside me. **I met her in a hotel lobby masturbating with a magazine.**

And in the room, there was the pink and the green of my grandmother's sorority, the black and gold of my grandfather's Alpha brothers—gray-haired and straight-backed, flashing gold-capped teeth and baritone **A-Phi-A!** as I made my entrance. High-pitched calls of **Skee-wee** answering back to them. Another dream for me in their calling out to each other. **Of course you're gonna pledge one day,** my grandmother said to me over and over again. When I was a child, she surprised me once with a gift-wrapped hoodie, pale pink with My Grandmother Is An AKA in bright green letters. **That's just legacy, Melody,** she said. **I pledged, your grandfather pledged—**

Iris didn't.

A pause. Then quietly, her lips at my ear, **That's because your mama isn't legacy.**

This, I whispered back to her, quoting her sorority mantra, **is a serious matter.**

My grandmother laughed and laughed.

Look back at me on that last day in May. Finally sixteen and the moment like a hand holding me out to the world. Rain giving way to a spectacular sun. Its rays speckling through the stained glass, dancing off the hardwood floors. The orchestra's music lifting through the open windows and out over the block as though it had always belonged to the Brooklyn air. Look at me. Hair flat-ironed and curling over my shoulders. Red lipstick, charcoaled eyes. The dress, Iris's dress, unworn in her closet until that moment. Already, when it was time for her ceremony, I was on my way. Already, at nearly sixteen, her belly told a story a celebration never could. My grandfather's oversize dress shirts backdropping the baby fat still pouting her cheeks, the fine lanugo hair still clinging to the nape of her neck. Still, that afternoon, the years that separated us could have been fifty— Iris standing at the bottom of the stairs watching me. Me looking away from

her. Where was I looking? At my father?
My grandparents? At anything. At anyone. But her.

Earlier that day, she came into my room
as I pulled stockings over my thighs, at-
tempted to clip them to an ivory gartered
corset. These too had once belonged to
her—unworn, still boxed and wrapped
with tissue paper. The fragile stocking
struggling against being locked into
the garter—this I had learned from my
grandmother—and she from her mother
and on back—mine the only ceremony
skipping a generation of mothers showing daughters. This—the corset wearing, the garters, the silk stockings—was
as old as the house my father and I
shared with my grandparents. This rit-
ual of marking class and time and tran-
sition stumbled back into the days of
cotillions, then morphed and morphed
again until it was this, some forgotten
ancestor's gartered corset—and a pair of
new silk stockings, delicate as dust.

I guess you win this round, she said.
Prince it is.

I looked up at her. The evening before
she'd twisted her hair into tight pin
curls, and standing before me, she began to pull them loose, her thick reddish hair springing into coils down over
her ears. The baby fat long gone from
her cheeks, replaced by high, stunning
bones. I pressed my hand against my
own face, felt the same structure beneath my skin.

**I didn't know it was a competi-
tion, Iris.**

Once, a long time ago, she was Mommy
and I held her neck, her arms, her
belly tight with dimpled baby hands.
I remember that. How I reached and
reached and reached for her. **Mommy.
Mommy. Mommy.**

The dress, white and unworn, lay spread
out on the bed beside me. Behind it,

a framed poster of Rage Against The Machine's 1997 concert. My father and I went because Wu-Tang was opening. I was twelve then and the two of us yelled and rapped and cheered so hard, we both stayed home the next day drinking lemon-honey tea to nurse our sore throats. The poster was professionally framed—the red letters against a gray matte, the oversize black frame picking up the muted colors of the black-and-white photograph. Beside it, another poster. If someone said choose between your mom and dad, I wouldn't need to blink. Wouldn't stutter. I'd run like a little kid and jump into my daddy's arms.

Feels like it's always a competition these days. Somewhere along the way, I became your enemy. She pressed her hand to her throat and held it there, her fingers gently moving across her collarbone as though she were checking to see if it remained intact. A gold bracelet slid down away from her wrist. Tiny diamonds catching the light. I swallowed, at once envying and adoring all the ways in which the word **lovely** could refer to my mother. So strange still, how different we were.

I had given up on trying to negotiate the stockings into the ridiculous garters and was just sitting there staring at her, elbows on my thighs, hands hanging down.

I don't get it. This is my **ceremony and you're trying to be stuck about the music. You blew yours, remember—**

No, the baby in my belly blew mine. Remember?

Don't even, Iris. Then for a moment, like so many times before this, I lost the words. Watched them drop . . . No. **Dissipate** . . . from the air between us. **Dissipate.** The word had shown up on my SAT prep tests again and again until it landed in this room with us. Between my mother. And me. **Don't**

even. I didn't ask to be born. I didn't say—I didn't say do what you and my dad were doing. You could have waited.

Iris raised an eyebrow at me. **I know you're not trying to have some kind of abstinence conversation with me.**

You could have. There wasn't some rush to do what you guys did.

You mean have sex? Can you really not even say it? Sex, Melody. It's just a three-letter word.

I can say it. I just don't need to right now.

And if we had . . . waited, as you say. Where would you be?

You regret the hell out of me.

Don't curse. I don't regret you. I couldn't imagine this world without you in it.

Then what is it?

She came over to the bed, sat down on the other side of the dress, and ran her hand longingly over it. There were crocheted white flowers at the wrist. The attached train had alternating silk and satin panels. The seamstress had already been working on it for months before my grandparents found out Iris was pregnant. By the time she started showing, the dress was almost done and paid for.

I don't know . . . , she said more to the dress than to me. **It's Prince. It's my parents. It's your father. It's me. It's you already sixteen now. Where did all those years go? It's crazy.**

There was a catch in her voice I didn't want to hear. Didn't want to deal with. Not now. Not on **my** day.

It's just Prince, for fuck's sake! It's not like I'm asking to walk in to N.W.A. or Lil' Bow Wow—

Stop cursing, Melody. You're better **than that. And N.W.A., Lil' whatever . . . I don't even know what you're saying.** She didn't look at me, just continued to run her hand back and forth over the dress. We had the same fingers, long and thin. Piano fingers, people said. But only she played.

I'm just saying it's Prince. And it's my ceremony and he's a genius so why are we even still talking about it? You already nixed the words. Let me at least have the music. Daddy doesn't care. He likes Prince too. Jeez!

For too long we said nothing. There was something moving through me like a razor in my chest—I didn't know then if it was rage or sadness or fear. Maybe Iris felt it too because she moved closer to me, rested her hand on the back of my neck, and pressed her lips into my hair. I wanted more, though—a hug, a kindness whispered into my ear. I wanted her to tell me I was beautiful, that she

didn't care what music played, that she
loved me. I wanted her to laugh with
me about the ridiculousness of garters
and stockings.

But instead, she got up, went over to the
window, and pulled the curtain back.
She stared down at the block as she
freed the rest of her curls. It was gray
out, drizzling. Downstairs, the orchestra had arrived. I could hear bows being pulled across violins. Could hear my
grandfather playing Monk on the piano
and imagined his dark fingers, knotted
at the knuckles.

Do you like Malcolm?

She turned back to me. Her skin
creased at the brow, her eyes—eyes I'd
prayed for as a child, **Please God let me
wake up with Mommy's pretty am-
ber eyes**—red-veined now. **Please God
don't ever let me have eyes like her
eyes are right now.**

Malcolm? Sure. Yeah. He's still such a sweetie. She looked at me, her mouth turning up into a half smile.

What?

What exactly are you asking me, Melody?

Do you like him . . . for me? Do you think he's a good— I don't know.

I looked up at her. Who else was there to ask who had lived through it all? From beginning to baby. First kiss to hands on a body to sex. How did you even begin it? Keep it going? Wasn't it supposed to be now that she gave me the answers. Told me everything?

You guys have known each other since you were in diapers and he's always been . . . I mean, isn't he?

Isn't he what?

Nothing. Never mind. She put her hands up, surrendering. **He seems,** she said again, smiling. **You just don't seem . . . his** type.

Like you would know anything about him. Or me.

Like I said, I've known that boy since he was in diapers.

Yeah, Iris. Both of us were in diapers a long time ago.

We got quiet. Maybe all over the world there were daughters who knew their mothers as young girls and old women, inside and out, deep. I wasn't one of them. Even when I was a baby, my memory of her is being only halfway here.

I hid you from them, you know, she said—like she was looking into my head finally. Seeing something there. **That's how you got here. They were**

hella good Catholics back then, but you would have been dust.

From who?

Whom, Melody. It's whom.

I was starting to sweat beneath the corset.

Your grandparents. Your beloved grandparents.

You didn't know. You told me you didn't know.

I never said I didn't know. I said I didn't know what to do.

She stopped talking suddenly and looked at me. Hard.

Is your period regular?

What . . . yeah! What the heck, Iris?

She exhaled. Shook her head. **Okay, so if you have a regular period and then it just stops and it's not stopping because you're suddenly a super athlete or something—then you're probably pregnant. I'm just saying that to you in case no one else does—**

I covered my ears. **I'm good. Don't need to hear this. Not today. Not from you. Thanks.**

No one ever said it to me. That's why I'm saying it to you. We can talk about this. By the time I was four months pregnant, what I didn't know was that on the other side of pregnancy there was Motherhood.

Of course it was, I said.

Of course it is, she said. **I know that now.**

How could you not know— You know what— Never mind. I don't get you.

The orchestra was warming up with "Jeannine, I Dream of Lilac Time." I could hear my grandfather singing the words along with Malcolm's little brother. One voice high. The other low. One voice young and unsure, the other old and clear and deep. I closed my eyes for a minute. The song was older than everyone in the house. When the trumpeter picked up a solo and the music lifted past where the voices had just been, I felt like my ribs were shattering. There was so much in all of it. Just. So. Much. I wanted to say to Iris, **It all feels like it's trying to drift out into somebody's eternity.** But when I looked up at her again, she was biting the edge of her thumbnail, her left eyebrow jumping the way it did when she was stressing.

I told Aubrey, she said, moving her finger away from her mouth and studying it. **And then both of us made believe it wasn't happening for a few months. Because we were kids thinking that if**

we ignored it, it would go away. I hid you until I couldn't anymore, wearing your granddad's button-down shirts, telling him it was the style.

Did you want to miscarry me?

I was a child, Melody. I was younger than you are now! I wanted to see you born. I wanted to hold you. I was stunned that it was true—that you could have sex with someone and that sex could make another human.

I tried to imagine her in my grandfather's clothes. Everything about her was feminine and tailored and perfect. Everything about her felt the opposite of me. I could imagine me in my grandfather's clothes. But not her.

I wanted you. I wanted you growing in my body, I wanted you in my arms, I wanted you over my shoulder—

She got quiet.

And then the wanting was gone, wasn't it?

She shook her head. More time passed before she spoke again.

It wasn't gone. Just different. You're going to learn this. I mean, I hope you learn this. Love changes and changes. Then it changes again. To-day, the love is me wanting to see you in that dress, she said. **I want to see me in you because** Me **in that dress was over a long time ago. Sixteen was gone. Then seventeen, eighteen—all of it.**

I pulled the dress closer to me—lace over silk and satin, tea length, manda-rin collared. A tailor had cinched the waist and let out the hips. He'd lifted the hem to see if there was extra fab-ric there to lengthen it. When there was only just enough, he used satin binding over the raw edge to squeeze the last of the length from it. My grandmother was so proud of his work. As I stood in his shop turning for the two of them, the tailor nodded approvingly and my grandmother dabbed at her eyes.

Iris turned back to the window. Silent again.

I stared at her back. Maybe this was the moment when I knew I was a part of a long line of almost erased stories. A child of denial. Of magical thinking. Of a time when Iris and my father wanted each other in . . . that way. The something they were so hungry for in each other becoming **me.** Me so in love with her that as a small child, I cried whenever my father put his arms around her. Said, **She's mine,** and cried harder when they laughed. A long line of screaming fights leading to us here now. Sixteen years of one or the other of us pushing away. She had won. Not me. Now, here was this, her standing with her back to me, hair half-done, half slip and bra beneath her satin robe, a woman too often confused for my sister. Here she was, in all of her deep unknowing knowing that this was the place, this was the time to keep me here by letting me know how easy it would have been to stay fifteen. That the people I loved almost as much as I loved my own father would have determined me **optional.** Two words spoken early enough, **I'm pregnant,** would have meant the end of my beginning. The end of so many beginnings.

Her back was narrow and straight, her shoulders squared beneath the delicate satin of her robe. She was fourteen months away from her thirty-third birthday. The age Christ was when he died, hung up on a cross and left to slowly bleed. In school, we'd been asked to discuss this image—Literal or

Metaphoric. Truth or Fiction. It was Whitman who said, **Argue not concerning God.** At the time we were in ninth grade—new to our beliefs and the power of our voices. So we argued. But now I knew there were so many ways to get hung from a cross—a mother's love for you morphing into something incomprehensible. A dress ghosted in another generation's dreams. A history of fire and ash and loss. Legacy.

That evening, as the music lifted up, I made my way slowly down the stairs and into the crowded room. When I looked for Iris, I found her standing beside my father, him in black, her in dark blue. Her hand on the now flat belly that could have expelled me. As the orchestra lifted into "Darling Nikki," I took small breaths to keep tears from coming. I had not expected this—to feel the close of a chapter. The girlhood of my life over now.

Amen. The end. Amen.

Cameras flashed as Malcolm took my hand, led me to the center of the gathered circle where my grandparents sat, somber and proud.

This was their perfect moment. Another almost-erased history unaborted. And this house with its hundred-plus years. This house with its stained-glass and leaded windows. This house with its generations cheering, saying, **Dance, y'all** and **Ashé** and **The ancestors are in the house, say what?** I and everything and everyone around me was their dream come true now. If this moment was a sentence, I'd be the period.

This house and these people, I kept thinking. **This house and these people. Who the fuck were they anyway? I didn't know Iris.** But truly, did I know any of them? Honestly? Deeply? Skin, blood, bone, and marrow?

Malcolm put his arms around my waist, whispered in my ear, **We so dark and**

lovely, got them feeling all black and blue.

Look closely. It's the spring of 2001 and I am finally sixteen. How many hundreds of ancestors knew a moment like this? Before the narrative of their lives changed once again forever, there was Bach and Ellington, Monk and Ma Rainey, Hooker and Holiday. Before the world as they knew it ended, they stepped out in heels with straightening-comb burns on their ears, gartered stockings, and lipstick for the first time.

Now Malcolm lifts my hand as we begin a slow cakewalk while a trumpet blows Armstrong into the room. Malcolm smiles then winks at me, our legs kicking into the air then swinging back behind us. The rest of the court dancing onto the floor to join in—our teenage feet in sync, our hands lifting into the air. Look how beautifully black we are.

And as we dance, I am not Melody who is sixteen, I am not my parents' once illegitimate daughter—I am a narrative, someone's almost forgotten story. Remembered.

2

His daughter was descending the stairs. As the orchestra his in-laws paid for played, she was taking each step as though the world had stopped for her, as though this moment were the only moment on earth with her in it. And she was fine as hell—this girl, no, this **woman.** This seed of his, this cry into the night. This apology of a child, **Iris, I didn't mean to. Damn. I'm so,**

so sorry. When had it happened—her with so much of Iris, the cheekbones, the slant of the eyes, the smile with so much . . . what was that thing behind their smiles? Some long-held secret about **you.** Both of them knowing you, knowing what you'd been up to, as though they could see, taste, and smell it on you. Aubrey had seen that smile so many times over the past fourteen, no fifteen, sixteen years. Where were the years? And still.

And still, this moment with Melody walking toward them and this whack-ass rendering of Prince filling the house.

Aubrey leaned back against the wall, his hands felt unsure suddenly. Iris had hers pressed to her mouth. But what is the father of the child supposed to do with **his** hands? His big open hands. Where were they supposed to go when all they wanted was to reach out for this child, hug her, hide her from the world? These hands that had learned at seventeen how to snatch smelly diapers away from her tiny body, rub A&D ointment over her rashed behind, hold her until the stinging stopped. Until the crying stopped. Hold her—over his shoulder with his massive hand behind her fragile head, then on his chest, in his lap, in his arms, on his back, both shoulders, his hand on her shoulder as she scooted too fast away from him. . . . Who was this now, descending the stairs? This child he made and raised and loved. God, how he loved every single cell dividing. The coarseness of her hair, the deep vulnerable hollow in her neck, the half-moons beneath her nails. **Those show how many boyfriends you're gonna have. Watch out, world!** And her tears when they began to fade. **Does that mean no one's ever going to love me, Daddy?**

His baby girl was coming down those stairs and he was crying now, outright and silently, and no one had told him what to do with his hands. As he slid them into his pockets, Iris shot him a look. He pulled them out again, quickly wiped at his eyes. Clasped behind him? Against the wall? Arms raised, fingers laced on top of his head? Arms folded? What was the right thing? Why did he never know the damn right thing to do?

Always, there was this echo in his gut, this hunger for something not quite remembered but almost joyful. No, it **was** joy. Before Melody. Before Iris. When he was still a boy. In the half memory, he's walking behind his mother. Corpus Christi. Houston. New Orleans. Mobile. Tallahassee, the two of them following the coastline, always staying near to the water. It was an almost memory of the feel of the water. The smell of it. The warm foam against his bare feet. For so long, he believed it was the true ocean. He'd thought it neverending. And when he squatted to dig crabs from the sand, he'd thought he could dig to another country, step out of the sand on the other side, and meet boys his own age there. Chump dreams. Soft, childish dreams. He was a boy in cutoff shorts and a ragged T-shirt following behind his near white mother. That's all. And those nights when he woke up alone in the tiny apartments they'd found—over beauty shops and behind hardware stores and down long, dim, urine-scented hallways—he knew she'd gone off to meet up **with a friend** who she'd come home smelling of, pulling wrinkled bills from her pocket, then running a bath so hot, the bathroom floor grew slippery from the steam. Who were these friends? How come he never met them? Chump-ass dummy he was.

When he'd finally gotten the courage to ask—was he nine? ten? it's such a blur now—if his own dad had been a **friend,** his mother smiled such a deep and heartbreaking smile, he'd wanted to take the question back. Cut it into pieces. Make believe it wasn't now a part of the air between them.

Nah, Aubrey. Your daddy was free and clear love.

He liked to think about that. That two people had loved each other and made him.

He knew the story now. Now that he was a man. Now that he had his own child. His father was a musician, blue black and beautiful, his mother said one afternoon. Where were they living then? Another beach town, but where? He remembered that it was raining, but the rain was warm. His shorts were soaking wet and he was shirtless. Maybe he'd swum just before his mother said, **It's time for us to talk about the man who made you. Then I don't want to talk about it again. That clear?**

Maybe he'd nodded so vigorously his head hurt. He'd been hungry for this

story. For years and years he'd wanted it.
Once, as a very small boy, he'd reached
for the hand of a man who stood smoking on the boardwalk. The man was
tall, cream colored, and squinting out
at the water. Aubrey was stunned by
the beauty of the man's free hand—the
long fingers curling over the metal rail-
ing separating them from the water and
sand. His mother was gone. Maybe in
the bathroom. Maybe buying a loaded
hot dog for them to share—extra everything. Sauerkraut and onions spill-
ing over their fingers. Extra packets of
ketchup for him to nurse later, sucking
them flat. Whatever the reason, he was
alone with the man so close, Aubrey
could see the spray of dark freckles
below his eyes. Aubrey moved closer,
leaned his back against the rail. He'd
glanced up at the man as he slowly
walked his fingers closer, finally feeling
the soft skin moving over the knuckles. Maybe his mother appeared then.
He remembered her calling his name,
apologizing to the man, snatching at his

hand. Most of the rest of that memory is gone now. But soon after that—through the ebb and flow of his mother's words, in the **click click** of his nails being bitten down to the skin—he met his father.

He'd come to Santa Cruz with a jazz band, him on the trumpet. I think the whole university was in love with him.

As a man, he found the story cliché as hell, but as a child . . .

As a child so damn hungry for the meat it filled his belly with . . .

I was a senior by then, would be graduating in a month, and something about his mouth around that horn and his eyes on me. The way he saw me.

He remembered her looking out at the water. Remembered the two of them sitting in the damp sand, his head against

her arm. Warm rain coming down.
Flashes of memory like lightning. Flash.
Darkness. Flash. Darkness.

**I lost him for a while, though. After
we'd spent that week together, he had
to be somewhere on the East Coast
and I blended into the revolution for
a while.**

He remembered her sweet laughter.
How that day, there was such a sadness
behind it that he stopped biting and
looked up at her, startled.

**Then we met up again at Berkeley.
I'd decided I needed a graduate degree and he was still on the road with
that horn. So of course, there we were
together again, you know.**

He'd nodded even though he didn't
know.

**By then, though, he was high more
than he wasn't and I'd never been one**

for any kind of drugs or drinking, which made me a bit of an outcast.

She got quiet, wrapped her arm around him, and pulled him closer.

Heroin happened to him. Heroin made your daddy king of every party we went to.

For years and years afterward, Aubrey would remember that line, her voice moving over the word **hair-on** and him imagining the man that was his father pulling on a wig and making people laugh.

His father died before Aubrey was walking.

He had a place in Philadelphia some-where. I'd call and call and call and no one answered. Few months later, I was doing some research and decided to see what I could find out about him. Came across a small obit on

microfiche. He'd been dead nearly a year by then. Overdose. The end. Felt like movie credits going up a screen. Felt like a heavy curtain come down over me.

For a long time after that, they sat there, the rain falling over them, small waves lapping in, and every so often his mother's heavy sigh.

Her deeply tanned skin and dark gray eyes made people look at her, then look at him. She'd always kept her hair cut short, but that year it had grown into loose curls with so much gray and blond moving through it. They didn't match, the two of them. When he held his arm against hers and asked why, she laughed and said, **The black ancestors beat the crap out of the white ones and said, Let this baby on through.**

She said she'd chosen Santa Cruz because when she walked around the campus, she blended somehow, no one asking if she was part Negro, no one accusing her of passing for white. **It worked fine for me.**

With Melody, the ancestors had done a different dance, painted his child deep brown, then drew on all of Iris's features. He didn't understand genetics no matter how many times Iris tried to explain DNA. He didn't understand why everything didn't just blend into some new something instead of picking and choosing like it did. He wasn't smart like that. This, he knew.

Now out on the floor, Melody and Malcolm were being joined by their friends, other babies turned into teenagers becoming a crush of butt-length braids and perfectly shaped fades, long painted nails lacing into lotioned teenboy hands. He shook out his shoulders, realized his own hands were sweating. Most of the grown-ups were tapping their feet, some even moving in to dance beside the young people. He caught a glimpse of Malcolm's hand brushing over Melody's butt and something turned over inside of him. A new fear like a dragging bruise moving in his stomach. Were they fucking already? Not Melody. No. She would have talked to him. She would have given him something, dropped a few coins of info into his pocket. Yeah. His girl would talk to him before she did anything.

Wouldn't she?

He would give his own life to see Melody able to stay this young, to see her live her teenage life—all the years. He wanted to pull her to him now. Say, **Hold on to yourself, Melody. Don't get lost.** He wanted to say again what he'd said to her so many times before. **You're loved, baby, you're loved.**

Iris had come closer. He could smell her—cigarettes, patchouli oil, and cocoa butter. All those years ago, she'd come home from college smelling this way. Had come back different, further away from him and Melody, who at seven called her grandmother **Great Mama** and Iris, when Melody finally spoke to her again, **Iris.** She had left him and come back so far away, he found himself wondering if she'd ever truly loved him. But before he felt sure enough to ask her, she left again. Always leaving again. Still.

Still.

No one talked about this. His boys hadn't— The way it feels the first time you're inside a girl. Your own skin stretching back and holding you hostage just **that** far on the outside of pain.

He reached for her hand, biting his lip against the hurt of Iris not taking it into her own. After a moment, she wrapped her fingers inside of his, rested her head on his shoulder. Maybe this was right. Maybe this was who he was supposed to be right now. Melody's father. Iris's friend.

Now in the kitchen, he could see the caterers moving food out to the backyard. Bowls of red rice and beans, platters of BBQ chicken, a mountain of potato salad on a bright blue plate, miniature veggie, beef and chicken patties, pyramids of cornbread squares. Even a whole fish covered with peppers and onions.

He had spent his childhood on a diet of Reagan's cheese and Taystee Bread with the occasional roast beef boiled to chewing gum. His mother didn't care much about cooking, and on a good evening—payday or when her income tax return came in—the two of them sat at the table, peeling back foil-covered TV dinners, talking softly through mouthfuls of Salisbury steak and scorched mashed potatoes.

They had always been soft-spoken. Because they had always been afraid. Brooklyn was a new world they didn't quite yet understand—the angry Italian boys slamming into their shopping carts as they made their way to the A&P on Wyckoff Avenue. The elevated M train above their heads as they rushed to the check-cashing place on the corner of Gates and Myrtle. The thick women watching them from windowsills, their elbows propped onto dingy pillows, eyes slowly moving up the block, then down again. **Nosy as they want to be,** his mother said more than once. He never told her how they asked about his father. Was there one? Where was he? And even once, **Dark as you are, you sure you your mama's baby?** He didn't tell the women that he'd been born into a midwife's palms alone as breath itself—that in this new place, he felt himself becoming dust.

Once, a long time ago, he was a boy in yellowing T-shirts and sagging underwear. He was too skinny, his knees curling out from his ashy legs, his ankles and cheekbones sharp. When he remembers it, he remembers the hunger, a hollow pain in his stomach. He remembers the opening and closing of the refrigerator door. Again and again. Hoping that by some twist of the government or grace of his mother's ability to borrow ten dollars from a neighbor (**Go ask Thelma and tell her I'll give it back to her when I get my check on Friday**), there would suddenly be a package of bologna to fry up, some thin slices of American cheese, or a jar of mayonnaise and a couple of pieces of bread, even though he had eaten his fill of mayonnaise sandwiches. Some Saturdays, he woke to Spam fried to golden beside scrambled eggs and a chunk of fresh Italian bread from the bakery in Ridgewood where he and his friends snuck to some nights, reaching beneath the half-closed grate to steal warm loaves off the cooling rack. He wondered, as his hand reached into the bakery's darkness and clasped the bread, why the grate was left half-opened. Was there a science to the cooling? Or was this some small act of kindness from the Italian bakers—a gift to hungry brown children sneaking up to Ridgewood in the middle of the night.

He longed for Twinkies, Charleston Chews, peanuts—either Spanish or boiled, their softened shells echoing a South he vaguely remembered. His mouth watered for hot dogs slit down the middle and fried to curling, pancakes with salted margarine and Aunt Jemima syrup—his list went on.

Before he was a man who shaved and laughed with his head thrown back, he was a hungry boy, dipping his fingers into cans of Vienna sausage, licking at the juice that dripped down his wrist. The sink counter he leaned against dug into his spine. The linoleum covering it peeled up beneath a plastic dish drainer. Too often, drowned roaches floated in the pooled water beneath it. But once, a cardinal alighted on the kitchen windowsill and he found himself squinting long after it had flown away again, trying hard to hold on to its beauty.

I think we're all supposed to be dancing now, Iris said to him. **My parents are up.**

Is that what the rule book says? That's how this thing supposed to go?

Stop. She lifted her head off of his shoulder.

Stop what? I'm just asking.

No, you're just being passive-aggressive. She took her hand out of his, folded her arms, and looked away from him.

Now he was lost again.

3

The loneliness and the smoking both came during her sophomore year at Oberlin. Iris was living in a single room in Heritage House by then, the only all-black residence hall on campus. At night, as she sat at her desk hungrily bent over the pages of bell hooks's **Ain't I a Woman,** she could hear students hanging out in the lounge. Beneath the sounds of their flirting and laughter,

there was always music—LL Cool J and
A Tribe Called Quest on permanent
rotation, the beats moving around the
lounge and into her room. It was 1991,
and most days, walking the campus
alone, Iris felt like the years were rac-
ing by too quickly. Felt like she had so
much catching up to do with her life.
Saw a future with herself in it—alone.

On her desk, there was only a small picture of the three of them—her, Aubrey,
and Melody sitting on the stoop outside her parents' brownstone, Melody
on Aubrey's lap and her looking away
from the two of them—as though she
were already leaving them. Already
mostly gone.

It felt like forever ago that she and
Aubrey had spent nights dancing in
Knickerbocker Park as a DJ threw
down on two turntables and the crowd
yelled, **The roof, the roof, the roof
is on fire. We don't need no water,
let the motherfucker burn.** Her own

fist pumping into the air as she sipped from a brown-bagged forty-ounce and danced pressing her butt back against Aubrey.

Months before Melody was born, her parents bought the brownstone in Park Slope—a neighborhood as foreign to her as Mars, with its empty parks and whole swatches of neighborhood where she could walk for a long time without seeing any black people. They'd packed up and moved so fast, she'd barely had time to stick pieces of paper with their new address and phone number into the mailboxes of her friends. Park Slope was two bus lines away from her old neighborhood. On the morning they moved away, Aubrey cried and cried. But months later, his mother in hospice care, he was living with them.

She thought she'd come to Oberlin and make up for the friends she'd lost track of once Melody was born. She'd stuck her head back into her books with only one goal—to get into a college far away from everybody needing some part of her. But the kids at Oberlin seemed so much younger. Some had proudly talked about arriving virgins and their plans to stay that way until marriage. Too often she wanted to ask, **And what if the married sex isn't good? Then, you're a whole other kind of fucked.** Still, the people living in The House around her reminded her of home. Even the African students, the lilt of their accents rising up over the noise. Their laughter, the smell of the food they brought back from break and re-heated in the microwave—ackee and saltfish, peanut stews, garlicky greens and gumbos—all of it mixing with their own newly adult smells and filling The House. The Caribbean girls with their dark flawless skin and thick natural hair reminded her of the girls she'd gone to Catholic school with. Those same girls had known she was preg-nant before she even knew. **There's a baby in your belly, you know,** they'd whispered, circling around her. **We can see the way your busts are so big now and your butt rising like a balloon beneath your skirt.** How had they known—all of them no older than her but wiser already, older in some beyond years kind of way. A week later, she came home to find her mother sitting on the closed toilet seat in the upstairs bathroom, **her** bathroom, holding the box of unopened pads and crying. Then, even as she pressed her hands to her near flat belly, she knew. She had missed periods before. Periods were still new to her and they seemed to come and go as they pleased. But this was beyond the off and on of her period. Her body felt strange. Her nipples tingled even when Aubrey wasn't touching them. And in the early mornings, her mouth filled with a rank bile that had her running to the bathroom and then, afterward, left her too nauseated to eat anything.

This can't be for real, her mother cried into her hand, the box of pads limp in the other. **Please God in Heaven Almighty Father of mine, in the name of Your son and the Holy Mother, tell me I'm dreaming. Tell me this isn't how Satan is coming for us this time. No. Not my baby. Not my sweet, sweet baby.**

If there's a baby in me, Iris said quietly, her hands still pressing against her stomach, **I'm keeping it.**

And why the hell had she been so damn adamant? She'd never dreamed of being a mother. When she looked into her future, she saw college and some fancy job somewhere where she dressed cute and drank good wine at a restaurant after work. There were always candles in her future—candlelit tables and bathtubs and bedrooms. She didn't see Aubrey there. Aubrey with his dimple and his near white mother and the tiny darkened apartment he had grown up in. They ate margarine there, spread on white bread and topped with grape jelly. The first time Aubrey offered her margarine, she laughed. **You know that's not real butter, right?** But he'd just shrugged. **Taste good to me.** She couldn't see a future with someone who only knew margarine.

But in that moment, as her mother wept, she hugged her stomach and claimed whatever was growing there. She saw it all—a baby rising up inside of her, landing fully formed and beautiful into the world. She saw a child her parents couldn't try to control. This baby would belong to her. She hoped it would be born with Aubrey's deep brown skin and, maybe, her own amber eyes. Everywhere she and her baby went, people would stop, say, **Oh my God, that baby is so beautiful.** That's what it would mean for her, beauty around her always. Beauty constant as a beat. Beauty that was hers alone. She didn't love Aubrey enough to walk through the rest of her life with him. But she loved him enough to carry a part of him inside her, nourish it, love it, and see what it became. When he cried out in bed, begging her never to leave him, she couldn't promise she wouldn't. But she could hold him, stroke the back of his head, say again and again, **This is fun, isn't it? We're good together, right?** And now, she could say, **Look what we made.**

She hadn't thought she'd get pregnant. Most times, Aubrey wore a condom. When he didn't have one, he pulled out in time. Sometimes, she told him he didn't have to. She was young and hardly got her period, so whatever was down there that made it possible to have a baby wasn't even fully formed. She'd thought everything hadn't yet fallen into place.

You sure we're good? Aubrey whispered.

Of course I'm sure. What do you think I am, stupid?

Sitting on the toilet seat, her mother said again and again, **We're not that. We're not somebody's thrown-out trash like that.** And to God, she begged, **Please heavenly Father, tell me this is not Your plan for us.**

Now as winter began its gray descent over Ohio, Iris stared at her small stack of mail, a letter from home, **Essence** magazine, some offers for low-interest credit cards, and thought again about the many lifetimes ago since that conversation with her mother. Would the tragic comedy of memory ever stop replaying? Her mother flinging the box of pads, then lunging for her, screaming as she slapped and pulled at her daughter's hair. Iris wrapping her arms around her belly and sinking into a silent mass against the cool bathroom tiles. Her mother's fists and prayers pummeling down over her.

That afternoon, neither of them knew that Iris was nearly four months pregnant, already anemic and under-weight, and that for the next five months, the thing she'd crave over everything else was white bread slath-ered with margarine.

You're fifteen, her mother said, in tears now. **There's so much, Iris. So much more—**

It's not the end of the world, Mommy. It's just a baby.

Back then, that was as far as Iris could see—pregnancy, then birth, then a baby. She hadn't thought of the shame that would force her mother to move them out of Bushwick. Hadn't thought about the baby growing into a child and one day that child becoming her own age—and older than that.

Iris pressed the cold envelopes and mag-azine against her lips. **I was fifteen,** she whispered into them. **Fifteen. I wasn't even anybody yet.**

4

Even a man's gonna cry. You can't help it. The mind going everywhere. From the blessing of a new life coming and that thinking filling up your throat to your own daughter's childhood snatched right out from under you. Thought I would have Iris as a little girl longer than I did. But sitting here with you asleep in my lap, I can't imagine life any other way. Every moment for all the generations was leading to you here on my lap, your head against your grand-daddy's chest, already four years old. Hair smelling like coconut oil. Some-thing beneath that, though. Little-girl sweat—almost sour, but then just when I think that's what it is, it turns, sweet-ens somehow. Makes me want to sit here forever breathing in your scalp. When did your arms get so long? Your feet so big? These footie pajamas with reindeer all over them remind me of the ones your mama used to wear. She used to fall asleep on my lap just like this. Back at the other house. Oh time time time time. Where'd you go where'd you go?

My legs hurt tonight. Another place too—deep in my back somewhere, there's a dull, aching pain. I try not to think about it. Old people used to al-ways say, **You only as old as you feel.** Here I am closer to fifty than forty, but I feel older than that most days. Feel like the world is trying to pull me down back into it. Like God went ahead and said, **I've changed my mind about you, Po'Boy.** A bath with Epsom salts helps some evenings. Ginger tea keeps Sabe's good cooking in my belly. Sitting here holding you at the end of the day—that's . . . well, I'm not going to lie and say this isn't the best thing that ever happened to my life because it is.

Look at you laughing in your sleep. Got me wondering what you're dreaming about. What's making you laugh like that?

Tell your granddaddy what's playing in your pretty brown head, my little Melody. Name like a song. Like you were born and it was cause for the world to sing. You know how much your old granddaddy loves when you sing him silly songs? Sabe says she's gonna have to get some earplugs if she has to hear one more verse of "Elmo's World" or that song about how to grow a garden. But me, I can listen to your voice forever. Can't hear you singing enough.

Come a day when you'll hear Erroll Garner playing "Fly Me to the Moon" on the piano and your own sweet mouth won't know what to do with itself, baby girl. Lord. Lord. Lord. You got so much living ahead of you. I remember the first time I heard Etta James telling the world she'd rather be blind than have her man walk away from her. The way her voice . . . her voice, Melody. Like something maybe you're right now dreaming about. Wish I could sing it, but that would just wake you up crying. Hmph. Always wished I could sing. Wish I could move my fingers across the piano keys like Sir Garner— that man was a genius. And when he touched down on those keys and played "Jeannine, I Dream of Lilac Time"— man, step back! Ouch. Burn yourself just listening to it. Just listening. Just listening.

You haven't been on this earth long enough to understand, but one day you will. Trust your granddaddy on that.

It's a pretty night. I think the winter's trying to leave us. No more snow, but it looks cold out there. Our boy, Benjamin, was born on a night like this—cold and clear and quiet. That was when we were still in Chicago with Sabe's people. Feels like a long time ago, but not so far in the past that I don't remember the way that Chicago cold slipped past your **bones,** I swear. That wind coming off the water? What?! I don't miss Chicago. But I miss the time. I miss who me and your grandma were back then. Sabe with that belly and the two of us always so happy just to be near each other. The way a fire seemed to rise up every time our arms touched. The way she'd look at me like we had all the hours in the world to spend just grinning at each other. Yeah, I truly miss the time gone by.

But if we had stayed in that time, you wouldn't be asleep on me now still holding tight to that book about a rainbow fish. Wouldn't say this while I was reading it and you were awake, but I don't know about that fish giving all of its pretty rainbow scales away. Makes me think of your mama. Thought she was still ours. Thought she was still my little girl. But she wasn't. Thought one day she'd grow up and I'd walk her down the aisle and give her away. Truth is, though, she wasn't mine to give. Nah sir. She wasn't mine at all. But it felt like I'd been scaled alive when Sabe told me about you coming. Felt like someone had taken a knife to my skin and just lifted it up off of me. Guess that's where the tears came from, knowing that there's so much in this great big world that you don't have a single ounce of control over. Guess the sooner you learn that, the sooner you'll have one less heartbreak in your life. Oh Lord. Some evenings I don't know where the old pains end and the new ones begin. Feels like the older you get the more they run into one long, deep aching.

That night I got home from work to find Sabe in bed curled around a pillow,

I knew. Your grandma was never one to get back into bed once she'd gotten up. Get up. Make the bed. Start the day. That's who she was. Even after we lost Benjamin, she still got out of bed every morning. Moved slower with that new bend in her back and all, but still, she rose.

I said, **Sabe, you sick, sweetie?**

Your mind takes you places. Standing in our darkened room with only the light from the hall coming in, I thought maybe I was wrong. Maybe it wasn't what I knew but something scarier than that. Something fiercer. Your grandma holding that pillow like she was trying to hold on to life shook me.

But I knew. Quiet as it's kept, the connection between me and Iris was something nobody—not even me— understood. But I could look at your mama and know that she'd been with Aubrey in the same way that I could touch her shoulder and feel the hurting or the scared or the rage inside of her. I knew Iris in a way that Sabe didn't. But still.

Melody, I hope you never have to hear your daughter scream and cry to keep her baby. I hope you never have to stand in the home you thought you'd grow old in, knowing that the life you'd made with your wife and child was over. I hope you never have to rethink the actions of a God you'd always believed in. Me and Sabe didn't understand what we were supposed to do with this new burden. Then you were showing yourself. This round bump that used to mean Iris was about to have a growth spurt. Every few months or so when she was small, her stomach would do like yours. Stick out like somebody who hadn't left the dinner table soon enough. Then the next thing we knew, her stomach would be flat again and she'd be one or two inches taller. But this time, it wasn't about a growth spurt. That was you already inside her. Now look, you got your granddaddy crying again. Got this old man as misty-eyed as the day I first walked into that hospital room and saw your half-open eyes slide over to me.

I want to call her Melody, your mama said. **After Grandma Melody who almost died in Tulsa.**

After a moment, your mama looked square at me and Sabe and said, **But didn't die.**

Then she said your name again. Melody. And me and your grandma held hands and each said our silent thank-you to the same God we had come close to cursing only months before.

5

As Iris stood outside the student union, opening a letter her parents had sent—seventy-five dollars and a picture of Melody with it—the revelation of her pregnancy came rushing back at her. Her father's sobbing, her mother's rage, the nuns, the neighbors, and finally, their church. . . .

It seemed the longer she spent away from them, the more her family haunted her. Each week another letter, each month another picture of the baby that had come from her body morphing into a toddler, then a child. Now laughing. Now a forced smile. Hair in cornrows. Out and curling over her head. Pulled up into a ponytail of beaded braids. Iris could never look at her long enough. Wanted the hours alone to stare at the child's changing hands and now a new space in her mouth. In last month's photo, a front tooth dangled over her bottom lip and Iris laughed out loud, wanting to reach into the picture and yank the loose tooth from her daughter's mouth. She wondered about the conversations she missed with the child—the fights they must have had over Melody's need to keep that tooth a day, a week, a month, longer. Why hadn't Aubrey snuck into her room in the middle of the night and yanked it the way her own father had done—Iris waking in the morning with that new space in her mouth and a crisp dollar bill beneath her pillow. But now the tooth was gone. Had Melody gotten a dollar for it too? Iris studied the space—the pink half circle of gum beside a tiny front tooth that hung at a slight angle as though it too was loose now. Iris shivered. Ran her tongue along her own straight teeth. She had missed the child's birthday but had called, only to have Melody say, **It's my birthday and it's party day. Bye! Daddy got me a bicycle. Bye again.** And when she reminded the child that the bicycle was from both of them, Melody said, **But Daddy put it together. And Daddy's gonna teach me to ride.** Always the phone calls were **Daddy, Daddy, Daddy,** and TV shows she'd watched. When she tried to ask Melody what she was reading, the child laughed. **Everything,** she said. **I read everything.**

Now, staring at the picture of her daughter, she remembered again how her own mother had said more than once that there was nothing at all maternal about Iris and wondered if the maternal gene kicked in later. Iris wondered if it would happen in her twenties or thirties. And if it did, would she want more children? Definitely not with Aubrey. But if not him, then with whom? The dudes at Oberlin were so not the ones. Maybe she'd go to grad school. Meet someone there?

Is that your sister?

Iris jumped and the picture fell to the ground.

A girl she didn't know was standing beside her. The girl picked up the photo, brushed off the dusting of snow, and handed it back.

She's cute. She looks a lot like you.

Yeah. She does.

In the photo, Melody was holding an orange balloon and grinning into the camera—her hair neatly cornrowed, her eyes dark and clear. The hand holding the balloon showed perfectly manicured nails. Someone had polished them a pale pink. Emerald birthstones dotted her ears.

Iris, right? the girl said. **American literature. You debated Carver with that white dude. You won.**

Iris had no recollection of the girl being in her class, even though classes were small and it was easy to count the black kids. She remembered disagreeing with some guy about the brilliance of the writer. Carver's staccato sentences bothered her. They felt like something she could have written in seventh grade. But every white person in her class seemed to be in love.

How had she missed this girl?

Yeah, she said. **I can get with Márquez. At least the brother throws you an adjective or two.**

The girl smiled. She had small silver wire-framed glasses, her head covered with a dark green hood.

Iris put the money back into the envelope. Slid the picture of Melody into her coat pocket. She wanted to keep looking at her daughter—long and hard. Wanted to continue tracking the month's changes. See what parts of her continued to hold on, continued to connect them.

Jamison, the girl said, holding out her hand. There were silver rings on her thumb and middle finger.

Iris. Iris didn't know what to do after the handshake so she stood there, fingering the envelope and staring out over campus. Jamison took off her hood, and now, with her hair exposed, long locks tied back, Iris remembered her.

Yeah, you, she said.

Yeah, me. Jamison smiled. She took a package of Drum tobacco from her pocket and was now flicking some into paper. She rolled the cigarette expertly with one hand, lifted it to her mouth, and licked it closed. She smiled when she saw Iris watching her. Something about the hair and the rolling made Iris feel unsteady.

Melody's name had been her idea. **Whenever you say her name,** she told Aubrey, **it'll be like you're hearing a song.**

That's tight, Aubrey said. **I like it.** Then he kissed her. Again and again he kissed her.

Like the whiskey, Jamison said.

What?

My name sounds like the whiskey. I go by Jam here mostly, though. Like the jelly.

Can I try one of those? Iris pointed her chin toward her cigarette.

Sure thing.

It was early afternoon, two days into the long Thanksgiving weekend. Snow was coming down. Not the scary Ohio snow she'd witnessed her first winter here. This snow was gentler, more hesitant. From day one, Ohio had shaken her.

And it was shaking her again. Right now.

Jam handed her the cigarette. When she leaned in to let Iris light it against her own, Iris could smell her. She smelled like the cold and the earth and something deeply familiar.

You're from New York, right?

Yeah, Brooklyn. Iris took a small drag on the cigarette. The smoke tasted sweet and hot in her mouth.

Jam was tall, narrow-shouldered inside a green jacket and striped turtleneck. Her pants looked intentionally ragged—like she'd done work to get the fading just so. The girl's skin was medium brown and perfect—no pimples, no dark spots, no moles, nothing. Iris had found herself looking hard at people's skin. After she gave birth to Melody a crop of pimples erupted on her forehead, and for years they'd been coming and going. No matter how much she scrubbed and masked and steamed, she couldn't get rid of them. She took another puff of the cigarette, this time letting the smoke roll down into her lungs before exhaling. But this girl's skin—she wanted to touch it. Find out if it was as soft as it looked.

Been there my whole life, Iris said. **Till now.**

New Orleans, Jam said. **First gen. You?**

First what?

You the first in your tribe to go to college?

Iris shook her head. It was a question about class. She knew that now. It was the what-are-you question. The where and what and who do you come from.

Nah. She had learned how to answer it simply.

Aubrey wouldn't have been first gen either. But before she left for Oberlin, she watched from her bed as he rose at six every morning, changed Melody's diaper, brought her to Iris, then showered, shaved, and dressed for work. High school had been all he needed, he told her. **I'm good with a diploma and a job. Plus it's a Regents Diploma so I'm golden.** He'd been so proud of the gold seal attached to his diploma—a symbol of having done well on the exams in the five main subjects. If he had taken the SATs, Iris knew he probably would have scored high enough to get into any school he'd chosen. But he was done. He was **good.** Some mornings he whistled softly. Iris didn't understand his happiness. How this was so absolutely **enough** for him. After she latched Melody on to her breast, she pressed her nose into the baby's head and drifted back off to sleep. What she saw was a future past this moment of the three of them crowded into one bedroom every morning. A future bigger than the three of them living in her parents' brownstone. But more than that, she had never imagined Aubrey being the end of the line for her. An eternity with him had not been a part of her plan, whether or not she'd taken his cherry. As the acceptance letters started coming in, first Barnard, then Vassar, and finally Oberlin, she saw the chance to unrut herself. She saw the way out.

You miss her?

Who?

Your little sister, Jam said. **The kid in the photo.**

Yeah, Iris said.

You got others?

Iris shook her head. **No. Just her. Just Melody.**

Melody. That's a pretty name.

Iris smiled. They stood there shivering and silent, inhaling and exhaling smoke, watching it rise and vanish above them.

6

The first time Aubrey brought Iris home they were both fifteen, Iris with her hair in two French braids, greased-down **baby** hair arching above her brow and down the side of her face.

It's not baby hair, if you ain't no baby, Aubrey had said as he watched her work a toothbrush she'd pulled out of her bag and Murray's Nu Nile to achieve the effect.

Shut up. Iris laughed, pushing him away from her. **You're the one that's not a baby. Not anymore, thanks to me.**

It was summer 1984 and Iris had a copy of the paperback sticking out of her jeans pocket. Both of them had been blown away by the book—how Orwell had imagined something completely different from the year they were living in. It had made Aubrey love Iris even more—the thought of a world where he wasn't able to love her scared him. Still, Orwell had missed the important stuff—where were Kool and the Gang and Tina Turner and **Ghostbusters**? Where was Michael Jackson's **Thriller** dropping hard? If 1984 was anything, it sure as hell wasn't what Orwell imagined.

Iris was still living in Bushwick then and they'd spent the morning in her empty house, upstairs in her bedroom, where the bedspread matched the curtains and the walls were painted such a startling white, it looked as though they'd been done yesterday. Up in her room, they had lain on her bed kissing and rubbing against each other until Aubrey's lips burned and his body felt like it would explode from everything he wanted. They had been serious for four months, Iris hanging at the park while he shot baskets with his boys, then the two of them talking for hours on a bench in Knickerbocker Park, his hand beneath her shirt, warm on her back, her legs draped over his. What he felt for Iris was different from what he'd felt for other girls—when he was ten, eleven, twelve. This was deeper, older somehow—like a memory of something from a long time ago and them here now, inside that memory. She was always on his mind—in math class, at basketball practice, when he and his ma sat alone eating TV dinners—there she was, smiling at him, leaning in to kiss him, teasing him about his jump shot, his old-school PRO-Keds, his fresh haircut, the way his cheek dimpled just below his right eye.

I love you, he whispered into her ear as they lay side by side on her bed. **I love you so much, Iris.** Because maybe this was what love felt like—a constant ache, an endless need. He waited for Iris to tell him she loved him back, but instead, she reached inside his pants, then into his underwear, and wrapped her hand around him. He bit down hard on his bottom lip, closed his eyes, and waited for what came next. He was terrified of what came next. He had only done this to himself. His own Vaselined hand in the bathroom, with the door locked and water running in case he cried out to the images of girls he had only seen fully clothed reimagined naked playing in his head. He had imagined Iris naked, but no matter how tightly he closed his eyes, no matter how fast he moved his hand, her body was never clear. It was as though his own imagination waxed over when he tried to see her. Lying beside her, her hand moving slowly, his fingers moving up her belly and beneath her bra, he was grateful that she felt so surprising beneath her clothes. So perfect. When he opened his eyes again, Iris was smiling, that sloe-eyed smile that scared the hell out of him and made him love her more. She pulled his pants and underwear down below his knees, and because he didn't know what else to do, he closed his eyes again and let her. Praying silently that she'd stop. Hoping she wouldn't. **I love you,** he said again, because if he whispered anything else, he was sure he would cry. He didn't want to cry. He wanted to laugh. No, he wanted to cry.

Open your eyes and take my shirt off, she said.

He started unbuttoning her shirt slowly. In the movies he'd seen, this was part of the love scene, the guy looking into his girlfriend's eyes as he took off her clothes. He wanted this part to last forever. He wanted everything to be slow and perfect and right.

You mess around, my dad's gonna come home and find you in my room half-naked. Iris moved his hands away and quickly undid her own shirt. He didn't know what to do with his hands.

Take your clothes off, Aubrey! You acting like you don't want this.

He stumbled jumping off the bed, steadied himself against her dresser as he removed his pants and T-shirt. A fan whirred in the window, but the room was still hot. Other than the whirring, though, the house was quiet. He could hear his own panting as he climbed in beside her—so much excitement and fear. And then he was naked on top of her, just outside of her, and then, by some strange grace of God, he was inside of her. And that quickly, he wasn't a virgin anymore. That quickly, he had something to understand now—about how doing it felt. Painful. It hurt. Why did it hurt? But then the pain was gone. And it felt good. So good. So, so good.

But Iris wasn't crying.

The guys on the court said it hurt for girls the first time. They said there was some skin wall you had to break through. **Like a pearly gate,** they'd said. **And then you in Heaven!** He'd laughed with them, gave high fives as they lied about their first times. One brother went on and on about how this girl made him stop but he told her if she didn't let him finish, she'd have to walk around the neighborhood with a half-popped cherry and what kind of look was that. But they were wrong. There wasn't a skin wall, just Iris pressing up and him pressing down and the feeling like nothing he ever believed could exist on earth. His body exploding first inside of himself, then into Iris. He could feel himself shooting into her, her own body, swallowing him whole. This had to be love. It had to be.

After, as they lay there, their clothes quickly pulled back on, Aubrey wanted to ask her if there'd been some other dude before. But he couldn't. He wanted to ask if he was big enough, slow enough, good enough. She was smiling at him—that **I know something about you** smile, and he could only look away, out past the matching curtains and window fan, into the late afternoon. He felt like he had lost something. Something more than his virginity. Like something had been taken from him and he could never get it back. He felt like a punk thinking this. Iris had given it up to him. So why was he feeling like this? Why was he feeling like some promise the universe made had been broken? Damn.

An hour later, she was restyling her hair in front of somebody's side mirror—a banged-up Oldsmobile that had been abandoned on his block. For days before that, the car's presence embarrassed the hell out of him, but watching his girl do her thing with her hair to get cute for meeting his mama made him feel some other kind of way about the car. Like maybe some divine something had landed it where it sat, tireless and with a busted windshield, there for this very moment. The feeling that he'd lost something wasn't threatening to be tears anymore. But it was still there— heavy like that. He felt wet and sticky. He could still smell the two of them together. The guys hadn't talked about this—about how you smelled and felt afterward. Afterward, he had held Iris so tightly. If she hadn't said, **I can't even breathe right now,** he would have still been holding on to her, wanting to pull her inside of him. Even bent in front of the side mirror, just inches from him, Iris still felt too far away.

His mother was sitting in the darkened living room, the blinds pulled closed, the box fan on the floor blowing hot air around the room. She was wearing her robe and had two curlers at her forehead, the rest of her hair pulled back into a braid. Before Iris, the only love he truly had was for his ma. It was the truth about so many brothers. Especially on the court. Mothers were golden. One step outside the Mother Line and there was a fight.

Your mama is so—

Hey, man, don't talk about my mama unless you want me to fuck your ugly ass up!

But it felt different for Aubrey. The love he had for his mom was so deep, it felt like it belonged to an old man— somebody who'd been loving and being loved for decades. He loved everything about her—the way she smelled, still strangely of the briny water he'd known as a child, the way she danced alone some days when her oldies radio station played the Chi-Lites. **Oh, I see her face everywhere I go, on the street and even at the picture show.** He even loved her name—CathyMarie—two first names together, as though her parents had thought it was the most normal thing in the world to have another capital letter in the middle of your name. Cathy-Marie Daniels. When he was little, he'd wanted to be called AubreyBrown for no other reason but the capital B. He didn't have a middle name. Had always been Aubrey Daniels. But his mother refused to let him add the Brown. **Aubrey's fine,** she said. **Aubrey is perfect. You don't want everyone thinking your last name is Brown.** He let it go.

He had hoped to walk into the apartment with Iris hearing music and catching his mother dancing, deep in some memory, hips swaying, fingers silently snapping. But the darkness in their apartment signaled something different. Something that had been coming off and on for months now. The TV on more often. Her oldies station mostly silent. The curlers in the late afternoon, something always reeking beneath the scent of Lysol.

Aubrey stopped halfway into the living room.

Ma?

His mother didn't answer.

Oprah was on the television screen. He couldn't tell what the crisis was, but a white woman was sitting across from her crying. Oprah looked as though she'd soon start crying too. His own mother was crying.

Before Santa Cruz and Berkeley. Before the jazzman that was as close to a dad as Aubrey was ever going to get. Before she was his mama, she was a girl in Oakland, growing up in the system. For a long time, Aubrey hadn't understood what the system was but knew, by the way his mother's eyes darkened every time she spoke of it, that it wasn't something he ever wanted to be a part of. **Fuck around,** she'd said, **and your behind's gonna end up in the system.** Later on, he understood it had something to do with the ashy violent boys who came after him in school yards. Something to do with the sad-looking girls who walked through the halls holding their notebooks up over their chests. He knew the system was the white woman on the beach when he was seven years old who asked his mother why he wasn't in school on a weekday and the grocery store dude who side-eyed him, then asked his mother if she had any other foster children.

But the system had paid for college. And even for the short time that she'd been in grad school. The system helped cover rent and sent an envelope filled with brightly colored food stamps once a month. The system paid for the therapist his mama talked to when the system itself was coming back to haunt her dreams, she told him. But she never told him how it haunted her. **You don't need to know that,** she said. **I don't need to pass that down to you.**

On days when she was home from her part-time job in a mailroom somewhere in downtown Manhattan, he found her like she was now—in the darkened apartment with the TV on. **Erase, erase, erase,** he heard her whispering sometimes, gently tapping her hand against her forehead. **Erase it all.**

Once, because he had seen it on a television show, he suggested prayer. But she didn't believe in God. Or Jesus. Or Satan. Or prayer.

I believe in words, she said. **I believe in numbers and all the history I understand. I believe in things I can see.** When he was a little boy she used to hug him and say, **And man-oh-man how I believe in you, Aubrey. My love. My light. My life.**

My love. My light. My life. Aubrey stared through the near darkness remembering these words. Always he was remembering these words and the deep pain of love he had for his mama. And now that love had split and spread and grown. To include Iris.

Your mama looks like a white lady, Iris whispered. **'Cept for those curlers in her hair.**

She's not. She's black. Just light-skinned. He felt a sudden wave of annoyance. Maybe somewhere there was some whiteness in his mama, but if there was, she never talked about it and neither did he.

I brought my friend by to meet you, Ma. Her name's Iris.

Iris hung back behind him. He could see her trying not to look at the small darkened apartment with its folding table covered with a plastic cloth, coffee cups filling the sink, and an open jar of Maxwell House on the counter, spilled wet grains around it. A few wet-looking Cheerios circled the garbage can, a roach crawling over them.

His mother finally wiped her eyes and looked over at them. She took in Iris's hair, her tight T-shirt, and the jean shorts, and something in what Aubrey could see of her eyes against the backdrop of TV light flickered. Lit up. Then just as quickly dimmed again.

Fast nights make long days, his mother said softly. **That's all I'm going to say right now about you and your friend Iris.**

C'mon, Ma, Aubrey said. **She goes to Catholic school!**

And you know what they call people who went to Catholic school, right? She turned back to the television. **They call them Mom and Dad.**

Iris smiled, but he didn't find it even a little bit funny.

A commercial was on now—raisins dancing across the black-and-white screen.

Aubrey stood there, not wanting to go farther into the living room. Aside from the couch and TV, there were two straight-backed chairs, a small coffee table, and a dark green throw rug. Behind the couch, his mother kept two suitcases packed—one for him and one for her. They had always followed the water. But here in Brooklyn, now that he had Iris, he felt like he was where he wanted to always be. Felt like he was finally on truly solid ground.

It's nice to meet you, Iris said.

Nice meeting you, too.

They were standing in the hall separating the living room from his mother's bedroom. The apartment was a railroad, with one small room off the back where Aubrey slept in a single bed with a striped blanket made out of something that itched in the summer and wasn't even close to warm enough in the winter. Until he'd been inside Iris's house with its upright piano beneath framed portraits of ancient family members, he hadn't thought of him and his mama as poor. But now, in the dim room, with Iris breathing gently at his shoulder, he could see that was the case. He reached behind himself for Iris's hand. The strange thing was the shame that came with knowing this. He tried not to inhale the cheap Lysol smell, tried not to look at the vase filled with dusty plastic flowers.

I just wanted you to meet her before I walked her home, he said.

He went over to his mother and kissed her gently on the forehead. **I love you, Ma.**

The deep knot in his throat was the realization that from day one they'd always been in survival mode. Holding on. Clinging to **living.** Part-time paycheck to food stamps to part-time paycheck again.

Love you too, baby. Take one of these stamps and bring me back a Diet Coke. His mother pressed the stamp into his hand, looked into his eyes for a moment.

And use the change, she said, **to get you and your new friend a little something.**

7

As sure as my name is Sabe I'll tell you that if you want to survive, you have to put money everywhere. In your secret sewn-in coat pockets, inside those suede shoes you don't wear anymore but can't get rid of because they remind you of the years-ago time when you went out dancing on a Saturday night. You put your money underneath flower vases and candy dishes,

tied up in handkerchiefs stuffed way
back in your dresser drawer. You have to
know that the bank's not always going
to be open, might even say they don't
have your money anymore, and where
are you then? What have you got?

Listen. Those Tulsa white folks burned
my grandmama's beauty shop to the
ground! They burned up the school my
mama would have gone to and her daddy's restaurant. They nearly burned my
own mama, who carried a heart-shaped
scar on the side of her face till the day
they laid her in the ground. Imagine
them trying to set a two-year-old child
on fire. That's all my mama was—just
two years old and barely running when
the fire rained down on her. Her own
daddy snatching her up, but not before
that piece of wood from her mama's
beauty parlor landed on her cheek and
left its memory there all her life. Two
years old. Those white folks tried to
kill every living brown body in all of
Greenwood, my own mama included.

Every last one. That was 1921. History tries to call it a riot, but it was a massacre. Those white men brought in their warplanes and dropped bombs on my mama's neighborhood. God rest her soul, but if she was alive, she'd tell anyone listening the story. I must have heard it a hundred times by the time I was school age. I knew. And I made sure Iris knew. And I'm going to make sure Melody knows too, because if a body's to be remembered, someone has to tell its story. If they had burned my mama up, I wouldn't be here now. But I'll tell you this much—if I live to be a hundred and ninety-nine years old, I will never go to that state, as God is my Witness, my Savior, my Rock. You will never see Miss Sabe's foot in the state of Oklahoma.

The old folks used to say that from the ashes comes the new bird. There wasn't much they had left after the fires, but my mama's people packed up what they had and went up to Chicago, where my granddaddy's brother was a doctor. Even though Chicago had had its own troubles back in 1919, time had passed and my granddaddy's brother was doing well for himself. Married a nurse and they lived in a big house on the South Side. Fine clothes. Real silverware. Two kinds of meat every night. A maid. Lord. Sad thing was the nurse couldn't have children so among those four grown folks, my mama was their life.

Lord. Lord. Lord. Even with all that fine living, that fire stayed with my mama. Caught her up in the night as a child and woke her sweating and screaming. That's why I don't buy it when people say children don't know. That they're too young to understand. If they can walk and talk, they can understand. You look at how much growing a baby does in the first few years of its life— crawling, walking, talking, laughing. The brain just changing and changing. You can't tell me all of it's not becoming a part of their blood. Their memory.

Those white folks came with their
torches and their rages. They circled
in their cars, hollered out, called them
niggers like they were calling them
by their names. Turned my people's
lives and dreams to ash. So my mama
taught me all I know about holding on
to what's yours. I know you hold on to
your dreams and you hold on to your
money. And I know that paper money
burns, so you put it into rolls of quarters
and nickels and dimes. And when those
grow to be too many, you find the men
who sell you the blocks of gold. And
you take those blocks of gold and stack
them beneath your floorboards and way
up high in your cabinets. You let them
turn white with cold inside your freezer.
And every day you're living you tell your
child, **Don't let me die without you
knowing that throughout this house
is something for you. Something
you're going to need.**

From the time I could call her Mama
she was saying, **Sabe, you hold on to**

what's yours. Even with all these years on me I remember being a child and asking her about my teeth. Every time one of them fell out, I said, **Mama, this is mine. I'm supposed to hold on to it.** Makes me chuckle now. My mama—bless her heart—said, **You don't worry about those teeth. I got them. I'll hold on to them for you.** And somewhere in the world, I guess, there's a jelly jar full of my baby teeth.

I held on to my mama's Spelman College sweater. Wore it the first day I got there myself and still have it now. Held on to my own daddy's stethoscope until I pulled it out of its black leather case one winter and saw the rubber had melted into sticky pieces of nothing and the silver disk was flaked with rust. Seems all I had from them was the memories of fire and smoke. That and the gold all of them just kept putting aside for me. That gold, the way all of them—my grandpeople and mama and daddy and even my granddaddy's brother and wife—the way they all held deep to the belief that it couldn't be destroyed. That if you have gold, you're good for the rest of your life so long as you hide it.

All over this country people talk about a silver spoon, but truth be told, the spoon is gold. And solid. And stacked high and across. That's how you have to do if you're colored, black, Negro, brown . . . Whatever you're calling yourself that isn't white.

Lord.

But when your child shows up with a belly and she's not even full grown yet, you think for a minute that all those blocks of gold don't mean a damn thing out in the world if you haven't even taught your own child how to stay pure. How to hold on. How to grow into womanhood right. You cry into the night until your throat is raw and there's not another heave left inside of you. Not another drop of water left for your body to squeeze out. Not enough ways left to curse God and yourself. So even though you feel like you're never gonna get out of bed again, you rise. You decide you've had enough of the neighbors with their looks and their whispers and you rise. You keep your eyes on the priest when your own church people give you their backs on a Sunday and you rise. You rise in your Lord & Taylor cashmere coat and refuse to let shame stand beside you. And when the priest calls your only child into his chambers, rests his hand too high up on her thigh, and tells her about the place in hell that is waiting for her, you return only once more—to damn him. To damn them all. And rise.

And you keep on rising. Cash some of the gold back into money. Put the money into a house someplace far away from everything your child and you and your husband have always known about Brooklyn. You pack and you rise. You sing the songs you remember from your own childhood. **Mama may have. Papa may have . . .** You remember your parents living, wrap the ancient photos of **Lucille's Hair Heaven** and **Papa Joe's Supper Club** pulled from the flames . . . and you rise. You rise. You rise.

Every day since she was a baby, I've told Iris the story. How they came with intention. How the only thing they wanted was to see us gone. Our money gone. Our shops and schools and libraries—everything—just good and gone. And even though it happened twenty years before I was even a thought, I carry it. I carry the goneness. Iris carries the goneness. And watching her walk down those stairs, I know now that my grandbaby carries the goneness too.

But both of them need to know that inside the goneness you gotta carry so many other things. The running. The saving.

The surviving.

So after the tears were all cried out, it was time to move on and figure out what to do with all that was coming at me. I could do like I threatened—throw Iris out of my house and make believe she was never born. But who would that make me in the eyes of God? And in the eyes of my own blessed soul? Someone lower than every single one of those white men who torched my grandparents' lifework to the ground. And even lower than the white folks who laughed at the smoke and praised the flames.

So I rose.

Now my grandbaby is coming down the stairs we own. Wearing the dress I paid off more than sixteen years ago. Me and Po'Boy, we've bought our life back. We've scrimped and saved and spent to get what should have been ours out-right and always. What should've been everything my own grandma paid for. **Lucille's Hair Heaven.** Sounds like a place you can walk out of feeling like somebody's dream for you. **Papa Joe's Supper Club.** Can't help but imagine plates piled high with ribs and greens. Buttermilk biscuits and powdaddy, probably. Hot peach cobblers in cast-iron pans.

Listen. Pry that wood up from the bot-tom stair where her foot just landed. That's where the bars are. Even as a little girl she'd say, **When I jump on that stair, it doesn't sound like the others, Grandma.** Already four years old, knowing the dip and rise of sound so well that I picked up on her piano lessons where Iris had left off all those many years before. **Listen,** my grand-baby would say to her teacher, jumping off the piano bench and running over to the stairs, her braids swinging along her back and shoulders. **Listen to how different this step sounds from the rest.**

Then one night as I lay down beside her to read a good-night book, she looked at me wide-eyed and whispered, **The sound is because the other stairs are hollow, Grandma! But there's something inside that one.** Then she rose up, put her mouth close to my ear, and whispered, **Something hiding.** Maybe she was about five then. It was summer and Iris had decided to stay and work in Ohio, so it was still the four of us alone in the house. Most of the time, it was just me and Melody, with both Aubrey and Po'Boy working. And Lord, how me and her would walk. We'd walk and walk and walk, just the two of us. Every day we'd find something new to love in Brooklyn. I'd spent most of my life here, but it wasn't until Melody was born did I finally get to see it through her new smart eyes. Cardinals and flowers and bright-colored cars. Little girls with purple ribbons and old women with swollen ankles. She saw it all and showed me every bit of it. **Look at that, Grandma.** And that and that and that.

Then one day as we were sitting at the botanic garden eating some sandwiches I'd packed for us, the child turned to me and said, **Well, you're my grandmother and Iris is my mother, but you're like my mother and she's like . . .** Then she stopped and her little face got all frowned up like she was trying to figure it out. **I don't know what she's like, Grandma. She's like somebody who is never here with us.**

Then out of the blue, she said, **Does she have enough where she is?**

Does who, baby?

Iris!

God creates us warts and all and I look back on that beautiful day in the garden and my grandchild with her daddy's dark skin, her great-grandma's long, thick hair, and her own pretty, curious eyes. She'd been calling her own mama **Iris** for a long time by that point. Every time I heard her say it, it stopped me, made me think I should say to her, **That's your mama. Don't call her by her given name like that.** But I never did.

I didn't say it because she was a child who already knew what **Mama** meant. How and where mamas were supposed to be.

Iris has enough, Melody. All of us, we all have enough.

The stair, she said that night as I opened up the picture book she had picked for me to read. **There's something beneath it, Grandma.**

I didn't tell her then that what was there was the gold. The bars and bars of it. The money that would survive flames and water. And time.

Some of those white men were part-time friends of people. Separate as Tulsa was, people found ways to live their lives with each other in it. Until it got to be too much and black folks got to have more than white folks felt was right.

Now as she slowly makes her way down the stairs, I see the beauty and grace that is the child I tried to beat out of Iris and have to choke back a whole new kind of tears. Po'Boy puts his arm around my shoulder and I reach up for his hand. Feel the arthritis bending the bones in his fingers. Feel the thinness of his body that is cancer eating its way from inside to out and know I'll be growing old without him. No green drinks or raw diet or holistic doctor over on Flatbush Avenue seems to be helping him. Po'Boy wasting away. Pants half hanging off him even with the tailor on Fulton taking tuck after tuck. Now he's sitting here in his dark linen suit with his pretty blue shirt underneath and all of it hanging on him like it's being held up by air. I give his hand another squeeze and he pulls away to look over at me with that smile that says, **Don't even think what you thinking.** Smile he passed down to Iris and she handed on to Melody. Lord, I will love that man's smile till I die.

You feel like dancing? he asks me, and I nod. Because I know I don't have a whole lot more dances with him. I know the dance card God gave us is almost punched through.

And so me and Po'Boy rise.

8

I figure I got room in my heart for Sabe and Iris and my grandbaby, Melody. I even got room in my heart for Aubrey—more room after what came about with him and Iris. Maybe more room than I ever thought I'd have for him, but look at it. He's a child of God too. And we're supposed to be made in God's image but flawed. If I step back. If I look at Iris and Aubrey from the distance of common sense, I know they were just regular teenagers with hormones running through them that **they** didn't even understand. Animal instinct. Desire. Need. At this age, I could just as easily forget how close I was with my own johnson when I was young. Every chance I could get, I'd be closing the door to my room, telling my mother I was studying or reading or just needing a quiet moment.

When I got to Morehouse back in '62, I was a nineteen-year-old sprinter who had never been with a single woman. Wasn't like I didn't want to neither. I knew there were girls who would let you do things to them, but I didn't know them. My friends would get a little liquor in them and talk talk talk about those girls, but I didn't know how much was truth and how much was plain fiction. I did my work, ran my quarter miles, collected a few medals, and graduated with that accounting degree. I didn't have Olympic dreams or none of that. Just ran to run. Ran to feel myself breathing and the wind in my ears. Nothing is like a quarter-mile sprint. All muscle and breath and power. And then it's over and you got a thing behind you—another race you can clock among your races. Another medal sometimes. Another second or two off your time. Another year of the college paying your way. After graduating, I wrapped my running spikes in an old pillowcase and packed them away. Through Morehouse, I heard about a Negro firm that was hiring, so I took the bus over to it, got the job, and on the first day, the most beautiful woman you ever laid eyes on walked through the door asking after a cousin she was sent there to meet.

Shoot—I wanted to jump out of my chair and say, **Please, girl, let me be your make-believe cousin!**

I tell you, if I didn't think about finding that cousin and making him my best friend in the world, my name surely isn't Sammy Po'Boy Simmons.

Sabe wasn't studying me. Or sure made a good play at making believe she wasn't. She had a year more at Spelman and had to make up some courses that summer. I near about moved back onto the Morehouse campus and spent most evenings trying to walk where I thought she'd be.

There was the war going on, and as I watched so many of my friends get drafted, I thanked God every day for legs that let me run and the way my right eye looked out into the world without seeing it, a cataract at birth going unnoticed for too long. I thanked God for my draft rejection letter and for Sabe walking into that office.

Does it sound crazy to say I looked at her and saw the world falling into some kind of order that I didn't even know it was out of? She had a flash in her eyes—a spark of something solid and deep. All these years later, I still don't know how to talk about what I saw. But it moved from her eyes down around her cheekbones and on over her lips. Even in the bone straight of her back, you could see it. I wanted it with me, that thing she had inside her that I still can't explain. I wanted it—and Sabe—to always be with me.

Truth was you'd never met somebody lonelier than I was that year. I'd left my mama back in Brooklyn to go to a school I'd never seen in a city I'd never been to. It was my aunt Ella in North Carolina who wrote a letter to the president—Dr. Benjamin Mays—asking if he'd let me come to Morehouse. Dr. Mays wrote her back too, and next I knew, I was hugging my mama goodbye and boarding the Greyhound. I'd never given college much thought before Aunt Ella sent that letter. Some mornings I just have to close my eyes and thank God for the way He moves in His mysterious ways, cuz now, here we all are.

Thought I'd find work back home after college, but then that job came through. Much as I could, I called my mama, expensive as that was. Some days I just sat at my desk eating ham sandwiches and staring down at pages and pages full of numbers. Or I'd get off from work, put on my running shoes, and go over to the Morehouse track and just run quarter mile after quarter mile until all the air was gone from me and I stood there, hands on my knees, breath coming hard, my throat and stomach burning, the burning taking the place of the missing.

I'm staring back at more than thirty years gone by and lift my head to see Sabe standing in front of me, holding a textbook to her chest and smiling. I see the light blue skirt she's wearing and the white blouse. I see my Sabe's pretty black hair pulled back.

And then I hear her voice again. Soft-spoken. Some South in it. Some steel too.

Who are you running from, Mr. Jesse Owens?

How do you know I'm not running towards **something. Or someone?**

Some people don't believe that you can meet a person and know that's the person for you for the rest of your life. I'm not going to try to argue with them on that. I know what I know. I stood there grinning at the sound of her voice and my own answering it. We were married that following July 1967. At the house she'd grown up in in Chicago. On the most perfect day God ever gave to the world.

If Sabe had had her way, we would have stayed in Chicago with her people. As it was, we stayed on for a year until our first child was born. That was Benjamin. We named him for Sabe's daddy, who'd passed just before we got engaged. We don't talk much about any of that time. Benjamin's heart just didn't do what it needed to do and we got him baptized just in time to bury him. Prettiest baby you'd ever want to see. For the few weeks he was with us, he'd open his eyes and look right at you—like an old soul. Like it was somebody from the past trying to tell you something.

After Benjamin died, Sabe was ready for something new and we came here to New York, lived with my mama in the house she'd scrimped and saved and borrowed to buy. I got a job downtown and was able to help out. Sabe started teaching second grade at a Catholic school in the city and we'd meet and eat lunch together at Washington Square Park, watching the hippies and the comedians and the people riding bicycles. Sometimes we'd go to Prospect Park with my mama in the evenings and the three of us would put down a blanket and eat dinner there. Sabe and my mama'd drink tea and I'd have myself a Miller beer. When I remember those times, the sun is always shining and it is warm. But it must have rained. Must have gotten cold. And we must have spent a lot of that time carrying our sadness about Benjamin. Must have spent many nights crying into each other's shoulders.

We kept trying and praying for a baby, but it didn't seem like it was meant to ever happen again. I could see the pain Sabe carried, the way her shoulders dropped down some days and she went quiet.

I believe deep what they say about the Lord giveth and the Lord taketh away. The week we discovered my mother's liver had failed her and the doctors told us there wasn't anything they could do, Sabe realized she hadn't bled in two months. We spent equal time over the next months crying and laughing. Crying and laughing. My mama died at home with me, Sabe, and baby Iris at her bedside.

Let me see my grandbaby one more time, she said. And then she closed her eyes.

9

The night Iris fell asleep in her dorm room and dreamed of Aubrey's mom burning, she screamed out in the middle of the night. By then, Cathy-Marie had been gone for three years, so Iris didn't understand why the two— fire and CathyMarie—were suddenly haunting her.

The single bed was hard and foreign even all of these months later. She had doubled two flannel sheets over it, but could still feel the plastic mattress. And why? Were there really still bed wetters in college? And did anyone over ten years old still fit on a single mattress? She'd always slept in a queen-size bed. Hadn't remembered a time when she wasn't sprawled diagonally across it, her pillow pressed over her head to keep the light away. Even after Aubrey moved in. Her mother insisted he sleep in the guest room down the hall from hers until the baby came (which made zero sense to anybody and her mother knew that), but he'd tiptoe over to her room in the middle of the night and at eight, nine months pregnant, they found ways to have silent sex, the bed still more than big enough for both of them, belly and all, Aubrey's grief mixed with passion bringing a new desperation to the way he held her. By dawn, he'd be sound asleep in the guest room again and she'd have returned to her position—taking up the bed corner to corner.

It was springtime, her freshman year. The last of the snow had finally melted and there was something to the light in Ohio that made her want to never leave. As she stood at the window look-ing out, she felt even farther away from Brooklyn and everything she'd known. She had expected this feeling to be a stinging in her chest, a heaviness. But it wasn't. It was a freedom. A letting go. Even this early on she knew she could never be happy at home again. She had outgrown Brooklyn and Aubrey and even Melody. Was that cruel? To be the child's mother but even at nineteen have this gut sense she'd done all she could for her? She had given her life. Nursed the child all through junior and senior years of high school—running home at lunchtime to stuff food into her own mouth and her boob into the baby's. Each of them staring at the other in

wide-eyed amazement, as though to say,
How the hell did you get here? and
Are you going to stay? Her own body
growing another part—like a third arm
or second heart not quite beating in the
same rhythm. No—more like it was
beating against hers. Like it was knock-
ing at her own to the rhythm of **I'm
here. I'm here. I'm here.**

She could see some of her dorm mates
out on south quad. There was the African girl with the beautifully black skin
and even blacker hair that fell in twists
around her shoulders.

No master up in this hair, the girl had
said to her in class the first day, pulling her thick hair back into an oversize
Afro puff. Iris had not understood what
she meant and the girl looked at her
the way the Catholic girls had, a deep
knowing. Could she see that she was
a mother? That back in Brooklyn, she
had a whole adult life and Oberlin was
just a four-year moment already moving

too fast. But then the girl looked at her again, an up-and-down summing up of a look, and for the first time, Iris had felt the master all over her—her not-quite-light skin, her light brown eyes. Even her hair, the way it didn't spring into tight curls when wet the way Melody's and Aubrey's did but hung near straight in places, corkscrewed and frizzed in others.

Where are your people from? the girl asked. She was wearing a black T-shirt that had Zambia, Bitch! across it in bright red letters—answering her own question for anyone asking.

Brooklyn, Iris said. **Chicago before that. And a couple of ancestors from Tulsa.** Until then, she hadn't pulled Tulsa out of her pocket. It was a dormant history, her mother's old-fashioned story resurrected again and again with crazy-sounding talk about hidden money. And on the rare occasion when she'd had a glass or two of wine, her maudlin ancient despairing about—did it even really happen?—a massacre. How many times had her mother brought up the massacres when she was a child? Iris couldn't even count them. Then, at twelve she had shouted to her mother, **That's your history, not mine!** Her mother had gone silent, stunned at first, then a confusion that, to Iris's surprise, was followed by tears. **You're right, Iris,** she said. **It's not yours.**

But here, somehow, Tulsa felt like it could add a depth to her story. It was some foreign part of her set against the cosmopolitan of her New York story.

When I was a kid, the girl said, **I loved that play about Oklahoma. That song that went "Hush you kids my baby's a-sleeping . . . ,"** the girl sang, her lilt nearly gone, replaced by a twang that must have been a part of the play. Iris had never seen it. Had never traveled to Tulsa but knew somewhere deep inside herself that Tulsa was separate from Oklahoma—its own ghost of a place. It had something to do with the stories her mother kept trying to tell her as a child. Something to do with black folks and losing. Fire. Destruction of black futures. The words coming quickly now, playing like a bad jingle in her head. Vague memories of conversations with her mother. Black wealth something-something. The scar on Grandma Melody's head. Or was it cheek? Shoulder?

Now, watching the girl dancing out on the green with others, Iris remembered again how she laughed at the song, and the girl, sensing the laughter was directed at her, turned on her heel and walked away. She felt herself smiling again at the lilted twang—**My baby's a-sleeping.** Maybe it was in high school that you learned to make friends with other girls. But by the time she was in tenth grade, she was pregnant and dangerous. The Catholic girls had told her as much. **My mother says your belly is contagious. Pop. Pop. Pop. One two three. First it's you and next it's me.** They were fascinated by her. But from a distance, snapping their heads back toward the front of the classroom when she looked up to catch them staring, clustering in the bathroom and hallways to whisper about the hows and whens of her pregnancy. **I heard it was two boys at once. And that now she's got two babies in her belly.**

No, that's not it at all. I heard it was her own daddy that did it.

You lie!

Nope. It's true.

I heard there's another in she house. That she had when she was just eleven years old!

Impossible. It can't happen at eleven. Not to anybody.

Does she look like an anybody? If she got that one in her belly, she could have had another, I'm telling you. You don't even know how she got that one in there, do you? You don't know anything.

But did any of them know anything? She had wanted to jump into the center of their circles, belly and all, and tell them everything. How good it felt. How it smelled. How the sweat on Aubrey's neck tasted, the pleasure screams in the back of her throat that she had to swallow. She longed to shock the hell out of them with what she knew. Say, **Run and tell your mama about that!**

But before she could, the nuns were calling her parents into school.

It's not safe for someone in her . . . condition, they were told. Iris feeling small between them. Feeling her mother shrinking even smaller beside her.

You can arrange for someone from the board of education to work with her at home. She'll have to repeat this year given—

She will not repeat a year. It was her mother who finally spoke. **She is too smart to repeat a year.** And as the nun flicked her gaze across Iris's belly, her mother took her hand, rose, and pulled her up.

And even in her shame, she had held tight to her mother's hand, loving her more than she'd ever loved anyone in the world for pulling her away from the nun's gaze, for pulling her free.

There was no board of education. Instead, her mother loaded her up with textbooks and told her to study. But once her parents went off to work, Iris turned the television on, poured herself a second, third, fourth bowl of cereal, and sat watching game shows and soap operas.

There were pamphlets in the mail. Centers for GEDs, alternative schools for expectant teens, technical programs that promised blue-collar jobs upon completion with "No money down" and "You already qualify for student loans." With each letter addressed to her, there was a flood of sadness, of failure, of stuckness. In her fifth month, feeling overweight and ugly, she let Aubrey drag her back to his mother.

She knows, he said again and again. **It's cool.**

I see you and Aubrey wrote that check that your body's gotta cash now, she said, pointing her chin toward Iris's belly. The apartment was still dark, but cleaner, fresher smelling. The TV was off and his mother was dressed, her hair up in a braid on the top of her head, small, cat's-eye glasses around her neck.

He told me they kicked you out of school.

Iris nodded. His mother's voice was husky, years of smoking and maybe other things too. But she had quit, Aubrey said. And maybe those were the smells that weren't there anymore—cigarettes, ash, butane lighters. Pregnancy had made her sensitive to smell. Even the scent of something sweet baking could send her vomiting.

And both your parents working during the day now, so you're sitting around watching TV while Aubrey's at school. Iris could see now an old prettiness in Aubrey's mom. Something around the eyes. The way her hairline curved around her broad face. The slight smile—not quite a smirk, something kinder than that—that showed up when she spoke to her. **I'm sure the two of you are there fooling around when he's not.**

Iris didn't say anything but didn't drop her gaze either. It was true. The house was big, filled with moving boxes and draped furniture now. Most days, she was alone in it. Her mother had taken another job to stay ahead of the baby and the bills that would soon come with the house they were buying. **I'm getting us away from this place and these people. Fast as you can say Jack Rabbit, we'll be gone.**

Now here was Aubrey's mother offering her something else—study lessons. And company.

She wanted to be called CathyMarie and told Iris she would need to meet her at the library on Woodbine and Irving three days a week from eleven until three p.m. but that she should eat before she came and bring snacks to have while there. There was math and science to catch up on. There was Spanish and English—books to read, vocabulary to learn, evidence to cite, themes to analyze, essays to write.

She spoke slowly, carefully—as though she thought Iris weren't bright enough to take in what she was saying quickly. In the months that followed, Iris would realize she spoke this way to everyone, but that day, she could feel herself holding back from asking CathyMarie to pick up the pace of her talking. She didn't. Aubrey stood grinning at his mother as though she were his only light.

I don't know why you're doing this, Iris said. **You're not a teacher.**

But she's smart, Aubrey said. **Ma taught me to read when I was three, remember?**

Yeah—you've told me a thousand times.

All the times tables by the time I was seven, Aubrey said, as though those words hadn't come out of his mouth before either.

You're the one who's pregnant, Cathy-Marie said—again in her too-slow, too-deliberate way. **But you're pregnant with Aubrey's child. My grandchild. It won't be about you anymore soon. And the last thing I want my grandchild's mother to be is a high school dropout.**

It's my **baby,** Iris said. **I'm the one doing all the work. I'm getting fat for it and puking for it and not sleeping because of it.**

It's yours now, Aubrey's mom said. **But it won't always be.**

She smiled. Her smile was Aubrey's, open and slightly pleading, straight white teeth and Aubrey's same full lips. **I'm not letting you get stuck here. If I could, I'd quit the piece of a part-time job I have and work with you five days a week—this is that important to me. But we're already breaking off**

pieces of this damn system with food stamps and Medicaid. I don't want any more of the half-ass help they call themselves giving us. If I quit my job, I'd have to take more from the government. Shit won't fly with me.

Iris nearly laughed then. With her mouth closed and her hair pulled back, his mother was a white lady. But once she started speaking, she was blacker than Aubrey.

Fuck workfare and this damn government, CathyMarie said more to herself than to Iris. **I'm not gonna let you and Aubrey get caught up in their game.** Then she closed her eyes for a moment, pressing her pale fingers against them. **But damn, am I hella tired, Iris. Hella tired.**

Years later, when she was close to fifty herself and sitting alone in her apartment waiting for the phone to ring— for Melody to call to offer up a lunch

date or a walk in Central Park, Iris
would remember this day and understand that CathyMarie too was lonely
and already dying. That maybe she'd
figured out that this was what she had
to give—some time with Iris and the
not-born baby before she was gone.
Leave behind in Iris's learning some
part of herself.

The following day, they started with
English, Iris sitting across from her at
the heavy oak table in the near silent
library. When CathyMarie lifted her
eyes from the textbook and slowly ex-
plained adverbial phrases, Iris realized
that Aubrey's mother had been a young
woman once who'd probably spent time
in bed naked biting at her man's ear.
And months later, when she took Iris's
hand in hers and showed her how to use
her fingers to help with the nine times
tables—**You should have learned this
in grade school. You have to know
this like you know your own damn
name if you want to get through**

algebra—Iris felt a sudden crushing fear of failing. Something shifted in her brain then, something unlocked as if she were waking up. CathyMarie's hand pressing her middle finger into her palm and insisting that science and math and reading were as important as her own name was the key to the next thing and the next and the next. Her parents had never preached it this way—it was a given. **You will go to school. You will go to college. You will learn. You will get a job.** The nuns had always ended with God's promises for once she died. But she wasn't dead. And she didn't plan to be dead for a long time. These numbers and words and facts were about something bigger. About something beyond the baby leaving her belly. They were about living. Iris felt all of this sinking in. And now she saw herself leaving. And now she saw herself gone.

I get it, she said. **I get it now.**

They ate bologna-and-cheese sandwiches, barbecue potato chips, and Oreo cookies sitting on the library steps. Washing it down with Coca-Cola. Years later, Iris wouldn't remember what they talked about as they ate, but she'd remember CathyMarie's laughter, the shape and warmth of her calloused hands. And after Melody was born, when she was back in school (the neighborhood public school now, with its loud students and burned-out teachers), she easily pulled down A's and remembered CathyMarie telling her that she was smart, that her brain wasn't crushed yet by time and people hinting at her lack of possibility. **Go do something,** CathyMarie had said. **You don't have a single excuse not to. Nothing's haunting you.**

Iris wished she would have asked at that moment, **What haunts** you? By the time she was out of her own head and old enough to know this is what she wanted to know, CathyMarie had been dead for years.

By Easter of that year, CathyMarie was in hospice care. Cancer in her liver, lungs, and marrow had withered her to pale skin holding tight to bone. By then it was too late for anyone to hold on to any part of her. Even Iris, who at nearly eight months pregnant, had come to love the way CathyMarie laughed, throwing her head back like Aubrey, and how she spoke of the power of water. **It always called me home, you know. Always beckoned to me. Still does. Some days I take the train out to Brighton Beach just to walk there. Just to be close to it. To hear it. Smell it and try not to feel so landlocked here.** When she said **unilateral** and **quadratic** and **coefficients** so slowly and carefully, Iris thought, **This woman acts like we have all the time in the world to get this algebra thing done.** All the time in the world. How little they both knew then.

Thirteen months later, Melody took her first steps across the sand at Coney Island, laughing as her tiny feet bent at the ankles, her dark brown toes sinking. Aubrey grinned as she walked toward him, holding his arms out for her to fall into. The wind blew her hair wild and this made her laugh harder. It was overcast and too cold for springtime, the beach nearly empty. Iris's parents stood bending into each other. Beside them, Iris held CathyMarie's ashes in her arms, cradling the box.

Isn't it early for her to be walking?

No. Because she's brilliant, Aubrey said. **We created a child and now here she is walking.**

Iris saw him glance at the box, then press his face into Melody's nearly non-existent neck. She watched him, wondering if her daughter's neck would ever grow long and thin like CathyMarie's. Aubrey seemed old now. So much older than seventeen. **How'd it get to be this?** he'd choked out that morning between bouts of sobbing. **I barely know your family and now it's all I got.**

He leaned over and kissed Iris, gently on the cheek, leaving the wet of his tears behind.

And now, Melody was pulling away from Aubrey and grinning with those few teeth in her mouth—tiny white perfect teeth.

Take one of these food stamps and go get me . . .

Iris blinked, stared out at the water.

We should do this, she said.

Aubrey looked up at her. Then nodded.

Aubrey carried Melody over to the grandparents. Then together, the two of them walked toward the water. When

Iris put her hand inside the box, Cathy-Marie's ashes were surprisingly warm. The wind lifted up as they sprinkled them—sending the white dust of her gently out over the ocean.

10

I too am singing America that morning in September.

Sitting at the Black Breakfast Table that becomes the Black Lunch Table at noon. Sitting between Malcolm and Leonard. Across from Clariss and Tenessa. Down from May and Nettie, whose real name is Wynett—how can a sister be given such a fucked-up name?

Wynett. After some corny-ass country singer and it's not like I'm trying to trash Wynett or her parents who I haven't met but I would like to see because I want to know what people who name a chocolate sister Wynett are thinking. And she's my girl so I don't mean any disrespect whatsoever cuz we all laugh at it. And we laugh loud. At everything. And give no damns that the white kids be looking at us like we don't even belong at that school, in their lunchroom, sticking tongs into their salad bars. Fuck no. Don't even know they're in the presence of royalty when they ask, **How come you all sit together?** without checking their own all-white tables. So we laugh loud, jump first in line on Fried Chicken Fridays, and eat it with our hands, even though I'm not allowed to eat it this way at home. I'm not at home, thank you very much. I am at this damn Country Day School that's not in the country and duh on the Day part. I am spending my years watching white girls snatch basketball-playing brothers into hallway corners and behind the pool and the brothers letting themselves get snatched.

They just want to know if the hair is as smooth below as it is on top, Leonard who doesn't play ball or get snatched tells the table. **Their mamas will slap them silly if they bring those Sallys home.** And we laugh. Loud. Watch the ballplayers sit at their own black table and the white girls blend back into their white worlds, tossing their hair over their shoulders. Tearing their chicken away from the bone with forks and delicate fingers. Eating it past the point where any of us eat it—where it's not cooked all the way through near the bone.

And when they ask us shyly—because they always do—if we're Prep for Prep or A Better Chance, we roll our eyes, smirk at each other in that way that brings color to their cheeks.

Nah, I say. **I got the same thing you got—grandparents paying cash money for me to go here.**

We say, **They think we all getting educated on layaway.**

And Malcolm, who rocks Prep for Prep, and Clarris, who's killing ABC, just look them up and down—from dirty sneakers to baseball cap. From polished toenails to ponytails.

We play Tupac loud, blast Jay-Z, Snoop Dogg, and Outkast as we walk in a black group away from the building at the end of the day, step into ol'-school dances like the wop and cabbage patch. We cheer on Malcolm voguing, his body moving like water. We laugh and curse loud on the train and watch folks choose another car and act like we don't give a shit that they're afraid of our Black Group.

But that morning in September, as we run from the Black Breakfast Table to the television in our homeroom, we blend into a single child crying as newscasters tell us how much we don't yet know.

Shit, we say out loud.

They're bombing us.

Jesus fucking Christ.

We say, **My father is in that building.** My mother. My sister. My brother. My uncle. My aunt. My grandmother. My grandfather. My friend. My father.

My father.

11

The first plan had been a road trip. The whole family piling into Po'Boy's Volvo for the eight-hour drive to Ohio. But Aubrey didn't drive and Po'Boy didn't think it was a good idea to subject a three-year-old to that kind of time in a car.

Aubrey tried not to look at Iris as he told Mr. Simmons that he agreed. Tried not to look at her too much at any point in the planning. The thing he had with Iris felt like a hole opening up in front of him. He wanted to know why she was leaving him. They had made something. No, **someone.** Together. And yeah, they had made **something** too. A family. A family that filled every floor of this house, spread out into all the rooms, echoed through the hallways, and yelled up and down the stairs. A family that splashed bathwater onto the floor as they lifted out of tubs. A family that wiped Melody's mouth and behind and swept up crumbs from around her high chair. A family that walked to the Häagen-Dazs on Seventh Avenue for cones and ate them sitting on their stoop. They laughed at Eddie Murphy movies, and on the now too rare occasion when Iris let him make love to her, it felt like their bodies were holding on to the earth. When he kissed her, he wanted her to swallow him, wanted to be all the way inside of her—his love was deep like that. And the family was the three of them, but then it was Po'Boy and Sabe too. And it was the people at their church who had watched them for years before seeing that they were good people, God's people, inviting them to picnics in the park and bus outings to the Statue of Liberty, Chinatown, Great Adventure.

Again and again he asked why Oberlin. Why so far away. Why was she leaving **them.** He asked what Po'Boy refused to ask. What her mother grew somber and silent about.

This is what we knew I'd do, Aubrey.

He knew what she wasn't saying. That the house felt small with him and Melody in it. Wrong. That she didn't want to live with him. Didn't want to raise anyone's child. Pregnancy was one thing, but being someone's mom was another.

He knew the long list of schools that accepted her had been her escape route. Oberlin was farthest away.

And what am I supposed to do for four years? he finally asked one night. **I'm just supposed to wait for you?**

She pressed into him, whispered, **I love you, Aubrey,** and he felt his body relax and grow hard at the same time. She was all he had now and she knew it. It was a strange power. **Jump for me, Aubrey.** And he jumped. Only after would he ask, **Why?**

They had grown. After Melody's birth. After his mother's passing. After her parents brought him into their house, they had grown fast. Aubrey shaving at sixteen. Gaining six inches by seventeen. Taking on a part-time job in the mailroom at a law firm that turned into a full-time job when they graduated.

He knew she hated that he found happiness in this—a job in the mailroom
of a law firm, their top floor in her parents' house, the baby crying until he
rose to comfort her. His being able to
do this. He knew she didn't understand
how this was enough.

In the end, she flew. Alone, the whole
family waving goodbye at the airport.
Melody in Aubrey's arms asking if she
was coming back soon. Matter-of-fact.
Like she was asking for a glass of water.
Like maybe it didn't really matter either
way. Then, in the next minute, burrow-
ing her head into her father's shoulder
and crying like the world was breaking.

And then there was the day during
freshman year when she had called to
tell him about her dream of his mother.
About the fire and how she'd screamed
herself awake. It was late in the evening,
long after he had put Melody down for
the night.

That fast, Aubrey, she said. **That fast some grandiose dream of a future can just . . . go out.**

He knew what grandiose meant but still tried to break it down in his head the way his mother used to tell him to do. Dios—the Spanish word for God. Grand—huge. It made some strange new kind of sense to him.

I miss her, he said. **I miss you.**

He could hear Iris softly crying on the other end.

I know, she said. **I know you do.**

He held the phone cupped between his shoulder and chin, pressing his ear into it. Wanting her closer, beside him. Even through the tears, though, he could hear the distance in her voice. Had it ever been anything other than this? He couldn't remember.

Every day it feels like I forget something else about being young, Iris was saying. **I tried to say the rosary the other day. Just to say it because I don't really care about it. But it was something I used to have to say every day all the time. I couldn't remember past "Hail Mary, full of grace." Even that chalky taste of the communion wafer. I don't remember how it felt on my tongue.**

He thought about her tongue. How soft and smooth it felt inside his mouth. He felt himself growing hard and told her. Sometimes she said things over the phone for him. Sometimes she'd talk in a way that made it feel like she was beside him, telling him what she was doing to him and how.

Everything, she said. Maybe she hadn't heard him. Her voice was lighter now, more distant. He wondered if she was high. **The wafting of incense through**

the church. Christ with his robe pulled back to show us his bleeding heart. Like Isaiah 54:7: For a mere moment, I have forsaken you. How come that verse is something I remember?

You know what I am now, Aubrey.

What? He had pulled the phone into their bathroom but now realized nothing was going to happen so leaned back against the sink and waited. He wondered if this was how it ended. If this was how people went their separate ways.

I'm a lapsed Catholic. And maybe that's why CathyMarie showed me the fire. She giggled and now he was sure she was high. He didn't ask, though. The thought of her there smoking weed with some dude he didn't know was too much to take in. It was close to midnight. He wondered if the guy was still there. Standing beside her, rubbing his hand over her back.

She got quiet. Then asked if he was still there.

Yeah, Aubrey said. **I am. I still am.**

But he knew she was the one who was gone. Iris. His first. **His** Iris had already left him.

12

The birth had been enough for two lifetimes—the baby's head feeling like it was trying to rip her in half, and then, if that wasn't everything, the shoulders coming next, broad and bony like Aubrey's. Worse than that, no one believed her screaming. The doctor saying over and over again, **It's just pressure you're feeling, the epidural is taking care of the pain.** She wanted to curse him out, stuff his body inside of hers so that he could feel this fire of a birth. This crap show of an experience. Pain like someone's Timberlands marching across her back while every other part of her burned and burned. Maybe this was the hell the nuns had warned of. Iris wanted to remind the doctor that his old white ass had never given birth so how the fuck would he know. But her mother was there, telling her to be strong, telling her she chose this, telling her it would be over soon. Rubbing ice chips across her lips. Saying, **I love you, baby. You can do this. You're my brave girl, Iris. You're my brave, brave girl.** She had given birth to Iris when she was forty. Benjamin dying only awhile after he had lived. She could feel her mother's fear that this one might not make it. Growing up in Chicago, her mother had known babies born without breath. Had known doctors slapping and aspirating and calling codes. Had listened to her uncle tell stories of teenage mothers losing their babies and sometimes their own lives. Her mother's hand inside her own trembled.

Jeez, she's a beauty, the doctor said. And then Melody was here in the world, red and wrinkled and crying.

Give her to me. She's mine. But as the nurse quickly wiped mucus and blood from the baby, then placed her tiny warm body against Iris's chest, the baby's eyes squinted open then shut again as though against bright light. Or maybe against Iris's own confused gaze. Iris felt a jolt of something, something electric and scary running between the two of them.

Fuck, Iris whispered. **Fuck.** If she were older, she would have been able to ask the bigger question—**What the fuck have I done?**

For days afterward, as nurses came and went, taking the baby and returning her with her shiny black hair neatly brushed to one side, Iris stared out her hospital window and saw the enormity of a life she hadn't even lived yet. The baby's eyes carried everything in them—they were almond shaped like her own, but for the few minutes they remained open, she could see that they were already a deep brown strangely flecked with green. The eyes were too beautiful. Too hungry. As they fluttered up toward Iris's own while she nursed, it was hard not to look back into them.

She felt like she was falling.

Each day, her sore and swollen body pressed against a hard wind blowing her own eyes closed. At night she went in and out of fitful sleeps, woke in the dark, sweaty and struggling for air. Where had the air gone?

Woke at dawn to find the baby still there. Swaddled. Blinking.

There was a new sickening perma-
nence to everything suddenly. At dawn
Aubrey showed up wide-eyed and full
of what can I do for yous just as she
was guiding her leaking nipple into
the crying, twisted mouth of the baby.
Even the nurse's hands, handling her
breast like no one had ever done, to
show her how to part Melody's lips
with it as thick pre-milk leaked onto
her still bloated stomach and hospital
gown. Even the tacky netted hospital
underwear and the oversize pad they'd
given her felt gross and never-ending.
Maybe she'd bleed forever. Be this sore
for always. Have someone needing and
needing and needing her for the rest of
her life.

Three days later, as Aubrey tenderly
tucked the baby into her car seat and sat
beside her in the back, nervously hov-
ering, Iris, slow-moving and still sore,
climbed into the front beside her father,
stone-faced and making plans.

You good? her father asked, glancing over at her.

Yeah. Fine.

You made a pretty baby, you know.

Thanks.

He drove slowly, Brooklyn streets inching past them. The baby slept and slept.

The weeks passed slowly. Day to night to day again, a long, unbroken line of the infant trying to suck the absolute life from her breasts while Iris sat in her parents' den looking through the college prep books her mother had started buying for her the summer before she entered high school. One arm holding the baby to her, she drafted letters on her parents' computer with the other one. Oregon, California, Ohio, and Washington State, the keys clicking beneath her right hand, the faraway states like a distant promise.

At night, as her breasts filled painfully again and again with milk that leaked through and stained her T-shirts, she lay in bed ignoring Melody's cries and studied trigonometry and chemistry.

As Aubrey slept with the baby on his chest, she read Shakespeare, the Brontës, Auden.

The desire was like nothing she'd ever known. Even as a child, she'd never doubted that she'd one day go to college. CathyMarie stoked something that had always been there, but Melody's birth—the pain of it, the absolute ferocity with which the baby pushed into the world—now felt like it had changed Iris's own DNA. But it hadn't. As her eyes burned in the dim light of the reading lamp, she knew it was her mother and her mother's mother and on back to something that couldn't be broken that was driving her. The story of her life had already been written. Baby or no baby.

She had missed the last months of tenth grade and the whole summer after that. She'd missed hanging with friends, smoking weed, and dancing to the DJs spinning in Halsey Park. Before she'd gotten kicked out of Our Lady of St. Martin, she'd found herself falling asleep in the middle of algebra, waking up because the teacher was calling her name.

Had it not been for CathyMarie, she would have ended up in summer school. Fuck Our Lady of St. Martin. Fuck summer school. Her brain was on fire, hungry as hell. The public high school was only two blocks away. She'd go there. She'd blow it out of the water. She'd leave here.

She was already mostly gone.

13

The first time his mother fell, Aubrey knew.

They had spent years walking beaches. The sand dipping and rolling uncertainly along the shore, deep holes that had been dug by dogs and shallower ones that sand and horseshoe crabs had left behind. Her feet had been pale, blue veined, and sure. Her toes painted purple, bright red, and he even remembers once, a glittering gold. No, she was sure-footed, his mother was. When **he** tripped, she looked at him like something had gone down strange in his brain. Like how could a kid who came out of her stumble like this. **Get up, Aubrey. And watch where you're stepping!** But she **never** had to watch her step. Her feet landed hard and firm and sure in the sand. Again and again and again imprinting it beautifully with tracks Aubrey stepped into, his own small feet sinking into the spaces she'd created.

So when she fell the first time, as they walked along the boardwalk at Coney Island, he knew. Her face landing hard against the splintering planks, swelling quickly as she lifted her head. Her immediate, **I'm all right, I'm all right. Don't make a fuss.**

Her hands scraped and bleeding from failing to stop her fall. Pants torn at the knee. A small crowd gathering but his mother trying to rise and scatter them. Her embarrassment clear as pain.

It was the beginning of spring. Had they been walking along the shoreline, the fall would have been a softer one. Or maybe there wouldn't have been any fall at all.

I'm all right, his mother said. **Just walk beside me slowly, Aubrey. Walk me on down to the water.**

14

They say you don't remember early stuff, that you're just suddenly six and having your first memories. But that's not true. I can go back to five and four and three. I can go back to thirteen and ten and six. But it's three that I'm remembering this morning. Three and Iris is nineteen. She's packing and I'm sitting in my daddy's lap watching her. The room is hot and thick—like there's another person in there with us or just something heavy. When I lean back against my daddy's chest, I can feel his heart beating. Not the slow beat I'd remembered falling asleep to. This was fast and hard. This was a terrifying pounding in his chest that I had to lift my head away from. Iris was humming as she packed. Every so often, she came over and kissed us both on our cheeks. She was happier than I'd ever seen her.

How strange it is to step back into that memory and see them there—my parents younger, my father thinner, my mother happier. The walls around us were painted a deep sagey green and the ceiling was white. That room didn't exist that way by the time I was ten. It had become the guest room that Iris slept in when she visited—a shell of a room with a full-size bed, a two-drawer dresser, and a small light clipped to the headboard. A room I had to dust every Sunday, with windows I was made to wash at the changing of the seasons. But then it felt full, crowded. My mother's suitcases and boxes of books, comforter, and pillows crowding it. My father and me sitting on the corner of the bed asking what we could do to help. Me handing her socks and bras and T-shirts. I don't think I understood what was happening.

Where we going, Iris? I asked again and again. **Where we going?**

Where are we going, Melody. It's where are **we going? Mommy's going to college to get her degree.**

At three, I didn't understand the word **college.** I didn't understand **degree.** That it would take four years. That four years would soon become **Forever.**

Where. Are. We. Going. Iris?

And then. And then. And then.

Sometimes the body shakes the memory off. I see my mother's suitcases being carried downstairs, her back disappearing through the door. My daddy's neck and shoulder rising up toward my face, toward my tears, my screams. My daddy's sides taking the blows of my kicking feet. His hands holding tight to me. My daddy. Holding on.

15

The winter Slip Rock's red Mercedes cruised up Cornelia Street, made a left turn on Knickerbocker Avenue, and faded into memory, Aubrey was fifteen years old. It was the first time he had seen a car like that in the real world. As he walked from his apartment with Iris's words still pressing against his brain, **You put a baby inside me,** he squinted at the pretty light-skinned brother he'd always kinda known now making good with his fly clothes and sweet ride. Slip Rock stuffed an unlit blunt into his mouth, then lifted his hand to his Kangol and nodded at Aubrey, his hazel eyes slitted against the winter sun.

What up, shorty?

What up, Slip Rock?

Ten years later, Aubrey stood holding Melody's hand and listening to an OG whose name he couldn't remember recount the story of Slip Rock's murder—**You know they shot him back of the head like they do when they real mad. That's how they killed that yella boy.** The old man's bottom dentures were loose in his mouth, moving in small circles as he spoke. Melody stared, her own mouth hanging open. Wide-eyed. The OG blinked down at her, then lowered his voice as he recounted the way the back of Slip's head was left dripping from the baby swings in Knickerbocker Park, his dookie chain snatched, his eyes blinked opened forever. **That's all she wrote,** the man said, folding his bottom lip in to steady his teeth.

Standing there, Aubrey remembered Slip Rock's nod, the cheeks still rocking baby fat and hardly anything on his face to shave yet. As the OG glanced at Melody again and took a sip from the bottle hidden inside a brown bag, Melody's eyes followed his hand, the bottle moving to his lips, the wince that followed the sip.

That your girl? Pretty lil thang. God'll make a butt-ugly boy, but I ain't never seen him make a ugly girl child. Now when they grown, well, that's a different story. The man laughed softly. Then took another drink and got quiet.

Forever, son, he repeated, as though he suddenly realized how poetic it sounded. **That boy's eyes was blinked open forever.**

Aubrey held tighter to Melody's hand, remembering how at fifteen, he'd watched Slip drive by, wishing he could get in the game, make some fast money, take himself and Iris and the baby that was coming away from this place forever.

Slip Rock had been spanking a royal-blue Adidas suit and blue Kangol matching it. He was about two years behind the fashion times, but it made sense—since he'd just done a stint at Spofford, where, as everybody knew, time stopped.

The speakers were blasting De La Soul and that was enough to bring all the kids on the block running toward the car. **Mirror, mirror, on the wall. Tell me, mirror, what is wrong?** But Aubrey stayed where he was, some distance

away from it all. He felt old, standing
there. A little bit broken. He'd fisted his
hands into the pockets of his pants and
could feel the lint at the bottom of them.
Even that saddened him. Lint instead of
cash. A tired pair of gabardines instead
of some breakaways. An old peacoat instead of a quarterfield. **You put a baby
inside me,** he heard again and again.
There was a baby growing inside Iris.
A baby. It felt like the whole world was
turning inside out on him. Crack had
killed and taken televisions and watches
and homes. As Slip Rock drove through
Brooklyn, everyone waving and feeling the jealous burn of his ride knew
crack had bought it. Crack had filled
his pockets with cash and put the heavy
gold chain around his neck. Crack had
bought him a gun and let him rent the
apartment above his mother's where
there was always a woman or two—fine
as the ones on **Yo! MTV Raps.** Crack
had paid for his fresh Caesar haircut
and the do-rag and the Murray's Nu
Nile Aubrey figured he used at night to

make the waves he sported beneath his Kangol. Aubrey bit at his bottom lip. All he had to do was nod back at Slip and he could get in the game.

You good? Slip called out to him. **Cuz you know I got you if you ain't.**

Aubrey felt light inside his sneakers. Felt like he could lift off, fly into Slip Rock's car, and be gone forever.

But he pressed his feet into the ground. Knotted his hands deeper inside his pockets. **Yeah,** he said. **I'm good.**

The phone had rung loud just after dawn, and as he put a pillow over his head to block out sound, he could hear his mother stumbling to answer it, then calling to him, holding the phone out. **Tell her not to be calling my house this early anymore. I thought somebody had** died! The cord not long enough to go beyond the kitchen, so him standing there, his mother too close, the air too hot around him. **You put a baby in me,** Iris said. His breath slowly leaving him. No air anywhere. His ragged underwear with the elastic shot around the leg holes, sagging like the rest of him. **But I thought . . . ,** he said. **I thought you said . . .** Inside he was screaming. **JesusJesusJesusJesusJesusJesus.** Inside he was crying out, watching his life—the rest of tenth, eleventh, twelfth grade, college ball—become a sinkhole beneath his PRO-Keds, become an airless room, his mother too close and all-knowing. **Nobody ever calls with good news this early in the morning.** And his own self fading.

How did ten years pass so quickly?

Is that where you kissed Iris for the first time? Melody asked him, her hand still in his, the OG gone now, stumbling down the block with the help of several front gates keeping him upright. Melody was wearing a green coat and white boots with the tiniest rise of a heel on them. He didn't know who had bought her those boots. They were too old for his baby girl. He didn't like the way they shaped her legs beneath her tights and lifted her feet off the ground just enough to promise something.

Did I tell you that?

You said you kissed her in a park and this is a park. What age is too young to be kissing, Daddy?

Twenty-one. Nah. Twenty-two. Actually, you shouldn't kiss somebody the way I kissed your mother till after I leave this world.

Daddy!

He squeezed her hand again and smiled. The sun was on them now, warm and bright against the cold. He'd never, ever imagined this—that he'd be bringing his daughter back to the old neighborhood. That so soon the old neighborhood would become heads blown off and stumbling old men. That his mother would be gone. And Iris . . .

You're never leaving this world, Daddy. Cuz then you'd be leaving me. I'm never leaving you and you're never leaving me. That's all she wrote.

Listen to you eavesdropping and repeating grown folks' conversations.

My friend Sasha, Daddy? She just lives with her mom. You should meet her mom and then me and Sasha could be sisters.

Aubrey laughed.

I know Sasha's mama.

You know her but not like that!

Now Aubrey threw his head back and laughed out loud, then looked down to see his daughter's own laughter. He had never imagined a love as deep and end-less as this. Melody unlocked her hand from his and wrapped it around his waist. She was getting tall, her knees, even inside her tights, sticking out like tiny knobs from her long legs. He wished she had meat on her bones, but he'd been skinny like this as a boy, and Iris, even as her stomach grew big back then, from behind, you could hardly tell she was pregnant.

Iris.

She had just turned twenty-five and was living on the Upper West Side now in an apartment owned by the parents of some friend from Oberlin. A pied-à-terre they'd abandoned for full-time life in Florida.

What the fuck's a pied terre, Iris? What the hell are you talking about?

Pied-à-terre. An extra apartment. She gave him that **how can you not know**

this look that burst into shame inside his chest. **They thought their kids would use it, but they all have their own places. They don't want to sell it in case some grandkids need a place to live.**

Fuck. White money is no joke.

Nope. It isn't.

The apartment was on the eleventh floor and the large windows looked out over Central Park. In real life this place would cost hella money, she'd told him. He'd stared out the windows, his hands clasped behind his back. A group of white women ran along the park, their ponytails bouncing out from the backs of baseball caps. He'd stood at the window watching this, wondering again when he'd lost Iris. Wondering again if she'd ever really been his.

On Saturdays, Melody stayed with Iris. Once in a while, when things were going well between the two of them, Melody would stay over an extra night, but most Sunday mornings, his daughter was blowing up his phone by seven in the morning, asking him when he was coming to get her.

Aubrey stared at the park bench and tried not to remember Iris with her legs draped over his, her tongue searching his mouth. He had always been too scared to ask her how she learned to kiss the way she did. He'd never asked her who was the first. Some things, he didn't think he wanted to know.

There was a mural to Slip Rock grinning out over the park—light-skinned and wide-nosed, his grin flashing gold-capped front teeth. Beneath it, in sprawling graffiti, the artist had sprayed Sun Rose: April 18, 1975 / Sun Setted: February 8, 1994.

Slip Rock. Gone.

Aubrey looked down at his daughter. Her grandmother had styled her hair into tiny box braids that curled at the edges and stopped just below her shoulders. She was staring out over the park, squinting.

That man's teeth shook.

Aubrey smiled. A deep orange light was filtering in through the branches, and something about the way it moved over the swings—too gently, too much like a caress—made something catch in the back of his throat.

It's poor around here, Melody said. **It's not poor where we live.**

Aubrey remembered the apartment he'd shared with his mother, how the linoleum peeled back over itself, revealing splintered floorboards and the black spots roaches left behind. What were those spots? Crap? Blood? He didn't know. His mother's hands had been calloused, but he never knew why. It had something to do with the system. The years she refused to talk about moving from home to home. It was the same reason that she refused to scrub their floors when he was young, and the one time he offered to do it—after Iris had come over, her eyes showing him the dirt he hadn't seen before—she told him her child would never scrub a floor. The fierceness in her voice, coupled with the sadness, scared him. But the first time he shook Sabe's and Po'Boy's hands, he was surprised. He had thought all grown-ups had rough and calloused hands. And now his own hand inside his daughter's felt the way his mother's had. Years in a mailroom, sorting and packing and opening. Years of crushing boxes and making binders and pulling staples before shredding documents. All of it had left him with a trace of asthma from the dust, and calloused hands. He wanted Melody to never have hands like his mother's. And maybe that was what being not poor was. They were not poor. Well, Melody wasn't. In a minute, he could be left with nothing. Iris had proved that to him. She had walked out that door and disappeared into a world he would never know. Left him in this one.

I can take a bus there to see you. Bring the baby, he'd said again and again.

But there was always a reason—exams, too cold, be home soon anyway. Always something that she offered up at arm's length—some **stay away from this part of my life** thing. Some **you belong in Brooklyn.**

You know what, Daddy?

What you got for me, Melody?

This place feels like from a long time ago. It feels like it's in the past tense.

Yup, Aubrey said.

Sun setted.

16

She was still beside her the next morning. It had never lasted into daylight this way. Mostly it was hurried and fraught—their want for each other so desperate, shirts had been left on, underwear ripped, legs cramped from standing. But for the first time, they had gotten naked, climbed under the covers of the tiny twin bed, and pressed into each other against the chill that

was still in the Ohio air. Iris lifted up
and stared down at Jam. Her locks were
spread over the pillow and across her
eyes. She traced her fingers over Jam's
breasts, down her belly, and into the
thick patch of black hair. Jam shivered
but didn't wake up. Iris leaned closer
and inhaled her hair. The locks smelled
like vinegar and heat. But there was
lavender too. She pressed her nose into
them, wondering if the smell of Jam's
hair would stay with her forever. Maybe
this was love—wanting someone with
all the senses. She leaned back against
her own pillow and closed her eyes.

When she woke up again, Jam's mouth
was on her breast, moving toward her
nipple. Iris jolted upright. During their
night of lovemaking, she'd been able
to keep the girl's mouth away from her
breasts, moving it instead back up to
her own lips or down between her legs.
Jam had smirked into the semidark-
ness but complied. But now, they were
both looking down at her breasts in

the bright daylight, milk seeping out over her belly. Iris tried to cover them with her hands, but Jam pulled them away, staring. When she looked into her eyes there were so many questions rising there.

It was nearly April. In another month, they'd be done with finals and heading home. Jamison back to New Orleans and Iris, for the first time in two years, home to Brooklyn. Maybe Aubrey knew. When they talked, there was such a pleading in his voice, such a hunger for her, that it came close to hurting. He was twenty-one now but still so fragile, so new about things. So . . . young.

Why's that happening, Jamison was asking. **Are they infected?**

They had been together nearly six months now—their relationship hidden from everyone at Oberlin, in Brooklyn and Louisiana. There was so much power in the not-telling, Iris thought.

It terrified her that they'd be found out, that this feeling, this none-ending wanting, would be brought to an end by anyone.

But there was something else. The slow falling in love with the way Jam's legs moved as she walked. The heat that rose inside her for Jam's hands slipping into the back pockets of her jeans. Even the jeans themselves—narrow-legged and low-slung while everyone around them seemed to be leaning toward pleated front pants rising over their navels. Once she walked by a classroom to see Jam in there with her arms slung back over her chair, smirking over the toothpick sticking out of the side of her mouth. Iris had spent the next hour wondering who Jam had been smirking at. But by the time they got together that evening, she'd lost the courage to ask. It felt crazy to even bring it up. Still, the way other students looked at Jam sent something moving through Iris. She didn't want Jamison's

eyes on anyone but her. When Jamison
laughed easily with other girls, Iris felt
like she was losing her. When she lay in
bed imagining someone else's mouth on
Jamison's, she had to take slow breaths
to calm herself down. She felt red at the
bone—like there was something inside
of her undone and bleeding. She wanted
this thing with Jam to last. Already,
she saw them growing old together—
Jam with her arm around Iris's waist in
the darkness. Days and days in bed together somewhere. Where—she didn't
know. It didn't matter, though. Not
now. Not yet. She wasn't gay or lesbian or queer or whatever else. It was
just Jam she wanted—her softness, the
way she laughed. The way she lifted a
cigarette to Iris's lips and held it while
she pulled. Watched as she exhaled
smoke, then leaned over and kissed her,
her eyes always slightly hooded, like
she had just gotten laid and was still
thinking about it. Jam she was in love
with and would be in love with always.

This naked, skin-peeled-back desire for someone was so new that it hurt. It felt too fragile—like Jam could turn to dust in her hands. Could walk away.

The first time Jam kissed her, she was unsteady for days. It was a Saturday and they had been outside Jam's dorm smoking Drum and watching white students, huddled together in polo shirts, smoke weed and dip their heads to Boy George. **Clowns caress you. Figures undress your fears. . . .** Jam had her head thrown back and was smiling. Something about the curve of her throat startled Iris. Earlier, they had finished their own joint, down-low passing it back and forth until all that remained was the roach burning between Iris's fingers. She had missed weed, and at Oberlin, even the lamest kids seemed to get their toke on. She thought it would be weak shit, but it wasn't. Staring at Jam's throat, Iris imagined her lips on it and laughed, blaming the weed.

Jam caught her looking and said—**I want to show you something in my room.**

It was a room she shared with a shy girl from Maine who spent most of her time at the library. Iris had only met the girl once but wasn't surprised to walk into Jam's room and see the child's bed neatly made, with a whole crop of pastel-covered stuffed animals arranged around her pillow and a Fleetwood Mac poster framed above it.

Jam's side of the room was all messy bed, Assata Shakur and Huey Newton posters. A row of well-cared-for Pumas lined the floor along her wall—black on white, gold on blue, red on black—the shoes went on and on. At the end of the line was one pair of Timberland boots. Even with all the sneakers, most times Jam wore the Timbs, and the sexiness of them was surprising.

There was a surrealness to it that made Iris giggle.

You still high? Jam asked, eyeing her as she pushed the door shut. In the tiny room, they were standing close enough to touch, and before Iris could lie and say no, Jam was kissing her, her mouth pressing hard into Iris's, her tongue insistent and sweet. They stumbled back against the wall and kept kissing.

I'm kissing a woman, Iris kept thinking. **I'm kissing Jamison!**

She let Jamison's hands explore her body but grabbed them when they reached for her breasts. Already, she could feel them leaking into her bra.

It's milk, she whispered now as Jam stared at her. Iris had pulled the covers up over her breasts and felt beneath them the milk seeping into her sheet. She felt scared suddenly. She couldn't look at Jam. Stared above her head, out the window.

She had nursed Melody for nearly three years. Not because she had to—she knew after the first year, the child got all she needed from her milk. No, she continued pulling to her breast first the infant, then the crawling baby, and finally the toddler because the milk kept coming and Melody kept wanting it. She nursed the child because she was supposed to feel some deep electric connectedness to her and didn't. So she gave her what she had—her body. This physical part of her, staring down into the child's eyes or into the pages of a textbook or, simply, out the window while Melody lay across her lap. And sucked and sucked and sucked.

When do I get those back? Aubrey teased, watching them. And she had smiled at him instead of saying, **Never. Not now. Not anymore.**

She thought once she finally stopped nursing, the milk would go away, that her breasts would shrink back to some normal size and she'd move on. But the first time Jam kissed her, she felt her

shirt growing damp, looked down to see
the familiar dark circles, and ended up
walking across campus with her books
held over her chest the way she had done
as a twelve-year-old—when her breasts
had first started growing and a band of
immature boys followed her home calling out, **Hey, Nipples, show us what
you growing.**

Melody, Iris said, jutting her chin
toward the mirror where a line of
Melody's pictures was tucked along the
side. **She's my daughter, not sister.**

Jamison stared at her for a long moment, looked over at the mirror, then
leaned back heavily, gently hitting her
head against the wall.

So you lied, she said after a long time
had passed.

If it had been Aubrey, she would have
double-talked, reasoned her way out
somehow. Turned his question around

on him until he doubted what he had always known. But it **wasn't** Aubrey. Jam was so different, so deeply on point and grounded. She was the only daughter of atheist college professors. She read Lorde and Baldwin and Nella Larson. She identified as queer, had a pierced nipple, and interrogated white professors. Her mind was sweet and sharp and she had an answer for whatever question came her way. Sitting in bed with her, Iris wondered if she'd ever had to lie. She doubted it. Jam said more than once, **Fuck this world. Ain't I a Woman.** It was months before Iris learned about Sojourner Truth. She had thought the "Ain't I a Woman" thing was Jam's own. Even their secret relationship—Jam had wanted to tell the world. Said, **Fuck this school, I don't care who knows what we do.** It was Iris who had wanted to hide, to keep it quiet. Just between the two of them.

And now, turning toward her, Iris realized that she had packed a suitcase full of lies and brought them all to Oberlin. Her leaky breasts were only one of them. The man she had at home. The school she'd gotten kicked out of. The baby she'd left behind. The mother who had beaten her and cried . . .

I did, Iris said. **Yeah, I lied. I had a kid when I was fifteen. That's her.** She pointed to the mirror. Melody at one, two, three, four, five. Each year pulling a little bit more of Iris into herself— eyes, lips, nose, smile.

But here you are fucking me? Jamison propped herself up on her elbow. **I don't get it.** Iris could hear students moving around in the hallway.

I like **you,** Iris said. She still could not look at her. When she looked down at her own hands, she realized she had grabbed bunches of sheet and blanket into them and was squeezing it so hard, her knuckles had turned a reddish brown.

What she was so afraid of saying was, **I love you. I want to be with you.** For nearly two years, she'd felt so much older than the other students at Oberlin. But with Jamison, she felt like a child suddenly. Wordless and floundering.

C'mon, Iris, Jam said. **You have a baby. Do you have a man?** She had risen to the side of the bed and was looking back over her shoulder at Iris. **Because I'm sure at fifteen you weren't trying to do some artificial insemination thing.**

The baby's dad lives with my parents.

So you mean he lives with you.

I live here, Iris said.

But you go home there. Jamison had pulled on a pair of white boxers and was pulling her jeans on over them. When she had buttoned the fly, she sat back down on the bed, shirtless. Iris wanted to reach out and touch her back. It was broad and dark brown and beautiful. How many other women had touched it, bit into it, pressed the side of their faces against it? She didn't want to know.

The milk had stopped running down. She would have to wash the sheets. The one time she'd tasted her own milk, she was surprised by the sweetness and had pressed some out onto her finger for Aubrey to try.

Can't I get it from the source? he asked.

Nope.

She wanted to tell this to Jam now— that she had only slept with him maybe a dozen times since Melody was born. That she didn't love him. That if they didn't have to use words like **gay** and **lesbian** and **queer** and **dyke,** maybe they could be together. If they didn't have to be public about it, maybe they could make this work.

But Jamison was pulling on her shirt—a flannel shirt cut off just at the waist so that when she leaned over to tie her Timberlands, a sliver of brown back teased Iris.

When she was fully dressed, Jamison walked over to the mirror and took a longer look at the pictures.

She's a beautiful kid, she said. Then she came back over to the bed, kissed Iris gently on the forehead. And left.

17

Now the house is quiet again, confetti vacuumed away, Iris back at her apartment in Manhattan, and the grown-ups who live here sleeping off the booze.

Some drunk ass spilled red wine on the side of my dress and now I'm seeing it for the first time. Malcolm on my

bed, smiling and high. Me thinking—
maybe this time we'll get it right.

Hey, he says.

Hey yourself.

Lou was drunk as hell, Malcolm says.
**I can't believe that cat can't hold his
liquor.**

He says things like that. Cat and cool
and dynamite.

He was dipping into the vodka hard.

I come over to him, give him my back
so that he can undo my zipper.

**What kind of neocolonialist shit you
wearing under there, girl?**

**Try neo-Victorian. It's a corset. Some-
thing old, you know. Like a wedding
but with shit that didn't really get
passed down the same way.**

Malcolm laughs. **Your family is bou-
gie as all get-out. I know I've said
this a million times, but damn. Today. Tonight. The whole thing.** He
draws exaggerated circles in the air with
his hands, shaking his head. He's gay as
hell, I know that. Anybody with eyes
and every person under twenty-one,
straight or gay, knows it. It's the grown-
ups who can't fathom what they refuse
to see.

**And then there was that old-ass
dude from your grandma's church
out there dancing with his lady and
trying to roll up on my ear. Talking
about** meet me in the car. **Like this
ain't Brooklyn. Like we gonna park
on some dark road. Like I want to
suck his wrinkled-ass dick.**

I free my boobs from the corset and
Malcolm's eyes get big.

Those girls are like, We're free, thank
you, Jesus! **Come on over here.**

I pull on one of my dad's old T-shirts—a gray one with Oberlin College in red letters across the front. It was the first and only shirt Iris brought home for him and stops just at my thighs.

Then I wrap my head and climb into bed beside Malcolm, let him put his arms around me from behind.

He cups my breasts and sighs. **In the perfect world,** he says, **these would be mine.**

The one time we tried more than cuddling was the only time I saw him cry. **I want to want you so badly,** he whispered. By then, we had been a couple for almost a year, Malcolm's arm around my shoulder as we walked around campus, his hand in mine as we headed with friends to the movies on weekends. But we both knew what we knew. Still.

You think it will ever happen for me, Malc. The sex thing.

**Shit, Melody. Hell yes and then hell
yes again. You're fuckin' beautiful
and . . . I mean, damn, ever since we
were little kids, I wanted to be you. I
wanted your hair and your butt and
your lips and your eyes and now—
look at your perfect-ass tits! Look at
your tiny-ass waist and**—he lifted one
of my hands, kissed the back of it gently—**I even want your perfect hands.
White boys can't see you and the
brothers just stupid, but you'll get
your fuck on. Trust.**

I turn toward him, burrow my head
into his chest. I can feel his heart beating against my forehead. Can smell the
Polo cologne he swears by.

**What about you, dude? What about
your cherry?**

He takes a deep breath. When he speaks,
he sounds tired.

**Sex is easy for a fag, girl. It's the love
I'm after. Bring on the love.**

Yeah, I say through a yawn. **The love.**

Today you got introduced to society, Melody, he says sleepily. **Shoot, I love that people think the world is even halfway ready for what we about to bring.**

18

Sitting here this afternoon, I'm thinking about that poem by . . . I think it's Dunbar, I'm not so sure anymore. Age will do that to you. Soon as something starts coming to your mind, it snatches it back. Makes you forget the stuff you want to remember. Brings back the memories you're busy trying to forget. This afternoon I miss Po'Boy and Aubrey so much.

Poem starts out, **Dey had a gread big pahty down to Tom's de othah night.** Just thinking about it makes me smile, you know. The way the poet played around with all those words—spelling them some other way than how they were supposed to be spelled but it making sense because that's how they sounded. I used to know that whole poem by heart. My mama would make me recite it when people gathered. Oration. I had wanted Iris and Aubrey to get Melody to remember it, but they said if she was going to recite anything, it was going to be somebody's rap song and none of us were having that. So we just settled for them going down to that dance school and learning the cakewalk and some of the other dances they did that night.

I like remembering the good stuff.

Something about memory. It takes you back to where you were and lets you just be there for a time. Five years to the day now that Aubrey died. Him like a son to me by then.

Was I dah? You bet! I nevah in my life see sich a sight.

It **was** Dunbar. I'm sure of it now. Paul Laurence Dunbar. My name is Sabe Ella Franklin and I'd like to recite "The Party" by Paul Laurence Dunbar.

We'd all thought after the cancer took Aubrey's mama fast as it did that Po'Boy would be the next one to go with the way it came for him just as bad and quick. Oh, how that man suffered in those last days, I can't even bring myself to— The thing is, I wanted to help him go. House set up like a hospital with his bed right here in our living room because he wanted the light. **That's all I'm going to ask you for, Sabe. Just put me where there's the most light.** So we put him here. And some mornings I'd come down and see him lying there looking out into it, crying. **I hurt so bad, Sabe. I hurt so so bad.** Those days I just wanted to crush his pain medicine to powder, mix it with orange juice, and help him slip into a deep sleep, then finally—on away from here. But I couldn't. Melody wasn't ready. Iris wasn't ready. The only one ready seemed to be me. I'd known all the Po'Boy this world was giving me to know. The man in the hospital bed was just Suffering incarnate. Just a shell of my Po'Boy. And that's what tore me up inside. But then he'd say, **Read to me, Sabe. I just want to hear your voice. Read me some of that Dunbar.**

I tell you, something about the poetry of Dunbar just made us laugh and laugh. Black folks trying to be all proper and speak like white folks and all. Used to get Po'Boy laughing when I read Dunbar's poems just the way the man intended them to be read. Used to make him go **You see how my Sabe do with those poems. Talented as she wants to be!** We both loved how he wrote. He was truly saying, **Can we just be who we are, people? Can we just take off our masks and laugh and dance and eat and talk?** But then he has the nerve to have that name Paul Laurence Dunbar—like you need to say it with your pinky pointing out. Hmph. Made me and Po'Boy shake our heads at all that our people are.

Lord, I miss Po'Boy. Miss him so much, Lord.

When I had my ceremony, I'd just turned seventeen, which is what they did sometimes. Sixteen, seventeen, eighteen. Some people waited till twenty-one, but after Iris got pregnant, I think I was nervous, and soon as Melody was born, I told Po'Boy we'd do her ceremony sooner rather than later. I should have known Melody would have been different, though. I should have known that sometimes common sense skips a generation.

I wore a white dress for mine. We always wore white. Melody tried to wear blue, but I shut that down. My own dress was tea length too and I had on white shoes that my mama had bought at Ohrbach's back when that store was still around. It was something to walk in there and have the salesman sit you down and take your foot in his hand. They took care with you. Put your foot up onto this inclined stool type of thing, then put that device underneath it. Made you feel so special. Then they brought you the shoes you had chosen in a few sizes. They really cared about their job. Made it seem like working with people's feet all day was the most important job in the world. But I tell you this. You walked out of there and you owned a pair of shoes that fit. Didn't have to worry about blisters or your heels getting torn up. None of that.

Two hours into it all, Melody said her feet hurt. Of course both Aubrey and Po'Boy told her it was okay to take off her shoes. Then it seemed every teenager on that floor was doing some cha-cha dance barefoot. They were done with the cakewalk and the Lindy and the waltz they'd been made to do. They'd gone from being proper to just . . . just dancing how they dance nowadays.

But before they started all that, those children were so beautiful on the floor.

Look at how the sun hits it now. All that gold on the yellowing pine and me here at the window—an old lady remembering.

Ike he foun' a cheer an' asked huh: "Won't you set down?" wif a smile.

An' she answe'd up a-bowin', "Oh, I reckon 'taint wuth while."

Dat was jes' fu' style, I reckon, 'cause she sot down jes' de same . . .

Oh, how the grown folks clapped when I finished my oration. My mama and daddy sitting right up front. So proud. So proud. Tickles me to look back and see Mama there, her beautiful hands clasped below her chin. Such a joy in her eyes. And beneath that joy, such a sadness. I remember looking up from my curtsy to see those near tears in her eyes. And then her quick shaking her head as though to say, **I'm okay.** As if to say, **Don't make a fuss about this or I'll tan your behind.**

Lord, I'm **tired.**

So many people I'm sitting here missing today. Lord, tell me what You left me here for. I feel like I've been alive so long, so long. Time for You to take me too.

I spend my days looking for signs. Today it's the light dancing across the floor. It's the squirrel with a piece of bread in his mouth scuttling up a tree. It's the cardinal on the windowsill. It's the bright blue car being driven by a blue-black man. It's Melody coming in from school saying, **Grandma, you've been sitting all day like that? Girl, let me at least take you out for an ice-cream cone.** And it's us on a park bench in the early evening. Sitting and licking. Sitting and licking.

From his place in Heaven, Po'Boy tells me to hold on. To just keep going a little while longer. Until Melody and Iris can figure each other out.

I'm old, but I'm trying. Hoping when I get to the gates, God will look down at His book and say, **You did good, Sabe. Come on home now. Come on home.**

19

I remember pushing through into the light. Into Iris's fear. Into the warmth of my grandmother's gaze. I remember hands on me. So many. And something warm being wrapped tight around me. I remember the pressure of something being cut from me, something from my face being lifted away, grease getting rubbed into my eyes.

A bit of the caul, my grandmother would tell me years and years later. **Over your forehead and left eye. I swear that nurse snatched it off and kept it.**

And I remember when they finally placed me at her breast, how I latched on so tight and hard, there was fear in her eyes. How absolutely hungry I was once. For her. For her. For her.

20

After Jamison left, I really did think I was going to die standing. No one had taught me this—how to get out of bed and keep moving. And for the few days afterward, each time I tried to, I stumbled, dizziness coming for me like a wave. The smell of her still so much a part of me that it hurt to inhale. No one had taught me how to eat. How to swallow. So I lay there—day moving into night into day, while in the halls, I could hear students doing what they needed to do. I lay there listening to laughter. To people calling each other by name. I lay there and heard showers being taken. Heard flip-flops moving through the hallways. Heard, **Yo, what's up with you?** And, **Hey, Byron, you take that test yet? Hit a brother up with some answers, man.** Heard, **Ooooh, I heard something about you last night, girl!** Heard, **What? What'd you hear? Who's lying on me now?** Heard, **We need to start a chapter of DST here. How they gonna not have any black Greeks.** Heard, **Check it,** followed by ciphers late into the night.

Slowly, Jamison's scent became my own funk. When I finally climbed out of bed, it wasn't so much to live. It was to wash and eat, to call home and hear a voice. To hear someone on the other end of that line who loved me.

Hey, Mom, it's Iris.

Hey, baby. How're you doing? Me and Po'Boy were just talking about you. Then the phone rings and here you are.

Can I speak to Melody, Mom?

When I saw Jam a few days later, she was lying outside on the green, her locks spread out around her head. There was a girl I didn't know sitting cross-legged beside her. The two of them were laughing, the girl's hand moving in small circles over Jam's belly. I stood there, watching them, until Jam lifted her head, looked over at me, and smiled.

Hey, Jam.

Hey, yourself. It's been a minute.

Yeah.

We good?

Yeah, I said. **We're good.**

If Aubrey had ever asked me, I would have told him there were so many before him. The first was a boy from my childhood when I was thirteen. He was pale as dust, with a perfect Afro and lashes that went on forever. I thought we were in love and we did it the first time up in his bedroom while his mother watched television one floor below. In our silence, as I gripped the pillow to keep from crying out in pain, I heard from below, **The survey says . . . !** Again and again. Followed by applause. But me and the boy weren't dating. We had never called what we were doing anything. So a week later, when I saw him walking with his arm around a pretty Puerto Rican girl, I crept upstairs to my room, faked the flu, and stayed in bed for days and days. Other boys followed and I learned quickly not to love them, to love the feeling of them inside me, the taste of their mouths, the way they held me. But nothing more.

That way, we were good. That way, **I** was good.

Cool. I bailed on that class, Jam said. **That's why you haven't seen me. It was bullshit. But we'll see each other around.**

She lay back down and went back to talking quietly with the girl. It was near the end of the school year. I had bought Aubrey a gray Oberlin T-shirt and a tiny one for Melody that said Future Yeowoman. Both were folded in the bag forgotten in my hand until I dropped it and heard the soft thud of it hitting the ground.

21

In the early morning, Melody and Iris sit in the big house alone, Iris in her mother's rocking chair, Melody at her feet on the floor. At the end of it all, Sabe talked about fire and gold. Fire and gold.

There had been a wake. A funeral. Prayers at the grave. Dirt sprinkled over Sabe's coffin. Ashes to ashes and we'll see you in the by-and-by as they lowered her down to join Aubrey and Po'Boy.

Then a repast.

The packing up of clothes and wash-cloths and winter coats. Sabe's shoes placed neatly in boxes for Goodwill. Her one wig that she wore to Easter service. Her kid leather gloves in black and blue and dark green. Pearl and gold chains to Melody. Her wedding band now on Iris's finger. Diamond bracelet they had both watched Po'Boy latch around her wrist the few times they went to the theater. Always for August Wilson plays. Once, a long time ago, to see a church production of **for colored girls who have considered suicide / when the rainbow is enuf.** Sabe returning in tears. **That woman can really tell our story,** she said. Then poured a small shot of brandy, threw her head back to drink it, and slowly climbed the stairs to bed.

It was early August now.

You ready? Iris asks.

Yeah, Melody says. **I was born ready.**

There had been a lifetime, a family, a new baby, a home. There had been so many after Jamison, after the first boy, after Aubrey. **Oh Aubrey,** Iris thinks now. **Oh Aubrey. I am so sorry.**

There had been the one night, only weeks after she and Aubrey first slept together, when she rounded the corner of Knickerbocker and saw him pressed against a girl she didn't know. His hands inside the girl's T-shirt, cupping her breasts in the darkness. When he cried, she forgave him. That was a long, long time ago. **Oh Aubrey. I am so damn sorry,** she thinks again. **If only we had known.**

Fire and gold and Aubrey to ash. The signs they'd posted for weeks and weeks. **Have you seen this man?** So many signs. So many people blown into history. But maybe he had survived. Maybe when the first plane hit . . . **Oh Aubrey.**

That morning, when Iris saw the smoke, she turned on the radio and listened. Then screamed and screamed as she ran—sixty blocks from her apartment on the Upper West Side, down Broadway, her throat burning, her heart feeling like it would stop. But it didn't stop. She ran until she couldn't see. Ran until smoke and dust and ash covered her. Until the police stopped her from getting any closer— and then she collapsed—at the corner of Thirteenth Street and Broadway, she collapsed. And all around her people were screaming and running and collapsing. Some deep and buried DNA ballooned into a memory of her mother's stories of Tulsa. She had felt this. And Sabe felt it. And she knew that as her child watched on the television in her classroom, she too felt the embers of Tulsa burning.

The rain is coming down harder, rivering along the sidewalk and dripping from the For Sale sign attached to a pole by the stairs. Save for the rocking chair and the boxes marked Fragile that Iris will be taking back to her apartment uptown, the house is nearly empty. Melody's suitcases, bedding, and poster of Prince are already in the car. The drive to Oberlin is just under eight hours.

Now Iris looks toward the window and remembers her mother getting out of a cab with a bag that seemed to be weighted down with bricks. Remembers her own pregnant fifteen-year-old self watching from her bedroom window, remembers the late-in-the-night hammering, her mother calling out to Po'Boy to make sure **everything's sealed real good.**

Then let's do this, Iris says now. She feels hollow. Untethered. She had thought freedom would feel different than this.

She walks over to the stairs, presses the crowbar beneath the bottom footbed, and waits for her daughter to swing the hammer. When she looks over at Melody, she sees for the first in a long time herself in the girl. In the way she lifts her head. In the way she is now leaning toward her, like a runner at the starting line. Ready.

Even if there's nothing there, Iris says, **you know we'll be okay, right?**

I've always been okay, Iris. Melody lifts the hammer. Lets the blows rain down. She doesn't have a whole lot of time for this. Malcolm is heading off to Stanford and there's a goodbye party for him in the city that evening. Outside, her friends are waiting. She lifts the hammer and again lets it fall.

And then it's there, amid the splintering pine and plaster dust. There beneath the sadness in her mother's eyes. There beneath the sound of her friends blowing the car horn and calling her name. In the empty house with everyone but the two of them gone now, there it is. Gleaming.

ACKNOWLEDGMENTS

Thanks to:

The Living:
Juliet & Toshi & Jana & Melanie &
Sarah & Jynne & Claire & Deb
& Dean & Donald & Nancy &
Kathleen & Linda & Jane & The
Family Dinner Crew & Odella &
Hope & Roman & Cass & Tayari
& Janice & Marley & Gayle & Maria &
Kwame & Jason & Chris.

The Ancestors:
Georgiana & Mary Ann & Robert
& Kay & Odell & Alvin & Anne &

Gunnar & Robin & David & Veronica & Hope & Grace.

The Future:
All the young people who are all the past & all the promise & all the gleaming.

Let the circle be unbroken.